‖‖‖‖‖‖‖‖‖‖‖‖‖‖‖‖‖

◁ **W9-BKZ-444**

"You have only to look as far as the medallion you wear around your neck to know the intentions of my father and yours."

At Eric's declaration, Brit stiffened. She felt for the chain at her neck and dragged the medallion out into the light. Her fingers closed around the warm, comforting shape of it. "What are you talking about? Your father gave me this for luck, to keep me safe from all evil, he said."

Eric was wearing that odd expression again—that sort of bemused half frown, his head tipped to the side. "You really don't know, do you?"

"What?" she demanded. He went on looking at her. She sad it again, louder. *"What?"*

And then, at last, he told her. "That medallion is mine. My father gave it to you so I might know you as my chosen bride."

Mrs. David Daute
5259 State Rd. 167
Hubertus, WI 53033

Dear Reader,

As you take a break from raking those autumn leaves, you'll want to check out our latest Silhouette Special Edition novels! This month, we're thrilled to feature Stella Bagwell's *Should Have Been Her Child* (#1570), the first book in her new miniseries, MEN OF THE WEST. Stella writes that this series is full of "rough, tough cowboys, the strong bond of sibling love and the wide-open skies of the west. Mix those elements with a dash of intrigue, mayhem and a whole lot of romance and you get the Ketchum family!" And we can't wait to read their stories!

Next, Christine Rimmer brings us *The Marriage Medallion* (#1567), the third book in her VIKING BRIDES series, which is all about matrimonial destiny and solving secrets of the past. In Jodi O'Donnell's *The Rancher's Daughter* (#1568), part of popular series MONTANA MAVERICKS: THE KINGSLEYS, two unlikely soul mates are trapped in a cave…and find a way to stay warm. *Practice Makes Pregnant* (#1569) by Lois Faye Dyer, the fourth book in the MANHATTAN MULTIPLES series, tells the story of a night of passion and a very unexpected development between a handsome attorney and a bashful assistant. Will their marriage of convenience turn to everlasting love?

Patricia Kay will hook readers into an intricate family dynamic and heart-thumping romance in *Secrets of a Small Town* (#1571). And Karen Sandler's *Counting on a Cowboy* (#1572) is an engaging tale about a good-hearted teacher who finds love with a rancher and his young daughter. You won't want to miss this touching story!

Stay warm in this crisp weather with six complex and satisfying romances. And be sure to return next month for more emotional storytelling from Silhouette Special Edition!

Happy reading!

Gail Chasan
Senior Editor

Please address questions and book requests to:
Silhouette Reader Service
U.S.: 3010 Walden Ave., P.O. Box 1325, Buffalo, NY 14269
Canadian: P.O. Box 609, Fort Erie, Ont. L2A 5X3

Christine Rimmer

THE MARRIAGE MEDALLION

Silhouette

SPECIAL EDITION™

Published by Silhouette Books

America's Publisher of Contemporary Romance

If you purchased this book without a cover you should be aware
that this book is stolen property. It was reported as "unsold and
destroyed" to the publisher, and neither the author nor the
publisher has received any payment for this "stripped book."

For those who never looked for love,
those who had more important things to do.
I do so hope that love found *you!*

SILHOUETTE BOOKS

ISBN 0-373-24567-X

THE MARRIAGE MEDALLION

Copyright © 2003 by Christine Rimmer

All rights reserved. Except for use in any review, the reproduction
or utilization of this work in whole or in part in any form by any
electronic, mechanical or other means, now known or hereafter
invented, including xerography, photocopying and recording, or in
any information storage or retrieval system, is forbidden without
the written permission of the editorial office, Silhouette Books,
233 Broadway, New York, NY 10279 U.S.A.

All characters in this book have no existence outside the imagination of
the author and have no relation whatsoever to anyone bearing the same
name or names. They are not even distantly inspired by any individual
known or unknown to the author, and all incidents are pure invention.

This edition published by arrangement with Harlequin Books S.A.

® and TM are trademarks of Harlequin Books S.A., used under license.
Trademarks indicated with ® are registered in the United States Patent
and Trademark Office, the Canadian Trade Marks Office and in other
countries.

Visit Silhouette at www.eHarlequin.com

Printed in U.S.A.

Books by Christine Rimmer

CHRISTINE RIMMER,

before settling down to write about the magic of romance, had been an actress, a salesclerk, a janitor, a model, a phone sales representative, a teacher, a waitress, a playwright and an office manager. Christine is grateful not only for the joy she finds in writing, but for what waits when the day's work is through: a man she loves, who loves her right back, and the privilege of watching their children grow and change day to day. She lives with her family in Oklahoma.

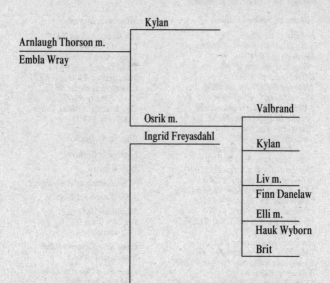

Arnlaugh Thorson m.
Embla Wray

Kylan

Osrik m.
Ingrid Freyasdahl

Valbrand

Kylan

Liv m.
Finn Danelaw

Elli m.
Hauk Wyborn

Brit

Davin Freyasdahl m.
Birget Larsen

Nanna m.
Cameron Briers

Gala

Brian

Kirsten m.
Alan Kervain

Ariana

Bronwyn

Brian

Chapter One

Princess Brit Thorson opened her eyes to find a blurry silver disc hanging directly in front of her face. Beyond the disc she could see the instrument panel of her Cessna Skyhawk.

She blinked. The metal disc still dangled, cold and heavy against the bridge of her nose, blocking the center of her vision. The controls were still there, too. Beyond them, through the windscreen now crosshatched with cracks, lay rocky ground. Farther away, steep black cliffs jutted downward, softened here and there with stands of evergreens, into a sliver of clear, pale blue Gullandrian sky.

It was cold and it was quiet—too quiet, except for the whispering whoosh of rising wind outside and various odd creaking noises all around her.

Her head hurt—and her arms were dangling over

her head. "Huh?" The world swam and shifted, her addled senses locking at last onto the correct perspective.

She was hanging upside down from the pilot's seat, held crookedly in place by her shoulder harness. The blurry disc? That silver medallion Medwyn Greyfell had given her before she left the palace on her way to the airport. "To keep you safe from all evil," her father's grand counselor had said.

Considering her current situation, the medallion could have done a better job.

Then again, though she hadn't made it to that meadow farther inland where her landing would have been much less eventful, she *was* alive....

Brit groaned and shut her eyes as it all came flooding back: the unremarkable takeoff from Lysgard Airport. The smooth climbout to 6500 feet. Once she'd reached cruising level, she'd banked right, heading northwest, following the curve of the Gullandrian shoreline. At the mouth of Drakveden Fjord, she'd made a right ninety.

And then...

That routine oil-pressure check. The reading: zero.

The awful, hollow feeling of unreality as she went about setting up her best glide speed, running through her emergency checklist, reminding her guide in the rear seat to buckle up, getting on the radio at emergency frequency to broadcast her call of distress.

And all the time, checking below, seeking some viable strip of land where she might bring the Cessna down in one piece. She'd sighted the narrow spit of dry ground at what seemed like the last possible second.

The landing had been rough, but they'd made it down okay. It was during the rollout that she lost it. Some jut of rock must have snagged a wheel. She remembered the sickening lurch, the right wing going up.

About then everything went black...

Brit popped the belt latch and crumpled with a grunt to the deck—scratch that: roof. With some effort, she untangled her arms and legs and got herself into a sitting position. She stared at the dead instrument panel and tried to get her foggy mind to focus.

The Skyhawk was a beautiful, soundly engineered piece of machinery. No way it would completely lose oil pressure out of nowhere—not without help.

Whatever had gone wrong, it wasn't by accident. Someone had tried to kill her. And someone had almost gotten what he—or she—wanted.

Gingerly she poked at the goose egg rising near her hairline. Hurt like hell. But other than that, now the disorientation was fading, she felt all right. Not terrific. Achy and stiff and bruised in places she'd never been bruised before. Also, a little too close to some serious cookie tossing. But passable. Once she and Rutland dragged themselves out of here, she should be able to keep up as the guide led the way to...

The thought trailed off unfinished. *Rutland.* When they boarded for takeoff, Rutland's long, lined face had looked way too pale. ''Don't care much for flying, Highness. Think I'll sit in back, if y'don't mind.''

After this experience, Rutland would probably never get in a plane again.

Brit shivered. With the heater as dead as the upside-down instrument panel in front of her, the cabin was getting colder by the minute. Outside, the wind kept whining and fading and then rising to whine again.

"Rutland?" Her voice sounded strange—strained and a little shaky—in the unnatural creaking quiet of the cabin, with the eerie wind whistling outside. She wriggled around, getting herself facing aft. "You all ri—" That last word became a tight, anguished cry.

Her guide was rear-end up, knees to the roof along with his head, which was pressed into his shoulders at an impossible angle. He stared at her through sightless eyes.

She'd got it right a moment ago. Rutland Gottshield would never get in a plane again—except maybe to be flown somewhere for burial.

Brit clapped a hand over her mouth. Very carefully, she sucked in a long, shaky breath through her nose. She let the air out. And repeated the process.

She wanted to scream. To throw up. To totally freak. To just give herself over to the sick, swirling combination of pity, panic and guilt that threatened to overwhelm her.

She swore low, and commanded herself through clenched teeth, "No. Don't you dare lose it. You keep it together."

Ignoring as best she could the dead eyes of her guide, Brit took a slow, careful look around. Both left and right hatches were crumpled shut. She moved back and forth, testing the handles. She beat on one and then the other, getting her shoulder into it. Neither gave so much as a fraction.

Okay, so she wasn't getting out through the doors. But she most definitely *was* getting out. And she was taking her pack, her coat and her weapon along with her, all of which waited aft—safe, she hoped—in the baggage net behind the rear seats.

Brit swallowed, sucked in another fortifying breath and wriggled between the front seats. Rutland was squarely in the way. As she tried to squeeze past him, his body crumpled to the side, landing half on top of her with a weird grunting rush of expelled air.

Deadweight, she thought with bleak humor. Never had the meaning of that phrase been so nauseatingly clear.

One deep breath. Another…

And then, with considerable effort, she pushed and prodded the body—still warm, oh, God—until it was rearranged into a marginally more dignified pose, resting against the battered side window, out of her way.

She collapsed the right rear seat back, got the baggage net unhooked and dragged out her stuff. Then, hauling it all along in front of her, she scrambled backward, slithering between the seats until she attained the cockpit area again.

''Weapon,'' she muttered, breathless, panting. It was wild country out there. Also, she hadn't fallen out of the sky by accident—and she'd do well to remember it.

Yes, she could shoot. Her uncle Cam had taught her, out in the vineyards of his Napa estate, years and years ago. And she kept in practice at a certain San Fernando Valley shooting range. When you lived and worked in one of the rougher areas of L.A., it never hurt to be able to protect yourself—whether at home or on the job. The job being the East Hollywood pizzeria where Brit waited tables to make ends meet.

The painful truth? Though Brit could handle a

weapon and fly a plane, she'd dropped out of UCLA—and somehow she could never quite manage to live on the income from her trust fund. There were always too many things she had to do. Flight lessons. Backpacking trips. Self-defense classes. Shooting range fees. And then, well, sometimes a friend would need a loan and she couldn't bring herself to tell them no.

Thus, the Pizza Pitstop had become part of her life. Paolo, Roberto and the guys always found it so amusing, when she told them to keep hands off or they'd be looking down the barrel of her trusty SIG 220. "Macha woman," they called her, chuckling with affection.

Not much to chuckle over now. Brit strapped on her shoulder holster, loaded her weapon and slid it in place beneath her left arm. Then she pulled on her thick down jacket. Barely September, and already it was major nippy in the Vildelund—the Vildelund being the Gullandrian name for the wild north country of her father's land.

Weapon loaded and ready, wearing her coat—unzipped, so she could reach the gun if she had to—her pack close at hand, she was ready to go.

Yet she didn't move. Cold as it was in the cabin, it would be colder still outside. She'd almost rather stay in here with her dead guide and the increasing chill and the creepy creaking sounds. At least in here she knew what she was up against.

She felt in a pocket, sighed in relief when she found they were still there: a full bag of peanut M&Ms. She liked to eat them when she was working at her laptop, writing one of the novels that always started out with a bang and somehow never got finished, or when she was feeling tense. Or feeling good...

Well, okay. The occasion didn't matter. She liked them, period. Some people smoked. Brit ate peanut M&Ms. She ate them one at a time—very slowly, sucking off the firm shell, getting to the soft chocolate beneath, never biting the peanut until all the coating was gone. She found the process of eating peanut M&Ms so pleasurable. And soothing—and comforting.

She could use a little comfort now. She pulled out the bag, tore off the top, took one out—a yellow one. She liked the yellow ones. Oh, hell, she liked all the colors. Even the greens.

She folded the top of the bag and stuck it back in her pocket and popped the single candy in her mouth. Umm.

Truth to tell, she could almost wish herself back in balmy East Hollywood, safe in her adorably seedy *Day of the Locust*-style courtyard apartment, tying up her duty shoes, ready to head out the door, late as usual for the lunch shift, looking forward to a few harsh words from her boss and an endless stream of—

''No!'' Brit sat up straighter, biting the peanut before all of the chocolate was gone. *Don't go there,* she commanded herself silently. *You wanted this. A man has died because you* had *to do this. You don't* even *get to wish it all away.*

And it was time. Time to stop cowering in the crushed cabin of her plane. Time to get a move on, time to be on her way.

Bracing between the upside-down seat and the un-budgeable hatch door, Brit kicked the windscreen's web of ruined Plexiglas out of the frame. That accomplished, she tossed her pack through the hole. And then came the fun part: dragging herself out after it.

As she crawled free of the wreckage, she marveled—better to marvel than to give in to the twin urges to burst into sobbing, desperate tears and start screaming in terror.

She was alive and that was something.

If only Rutland could be crawling out with her....

Shivering, her arms wrapped around herself, she crouched on her haunches on the unwelcoming rocky ground and stared through the ragged hole from which she'd just emerged.

Should she go back, try to drag the guide out, to give him the dignity of a shallow, rocky burial?

She shivered some more, shaking her head. To bury the guide would take time and considerable effort—both of which she needed to conserve at all costs. And Rutland wasn't going to care, either way.

Bracing her hands on her knees, she pushed herself up to a bent-over position. Whoopsy. Her head spun and her stomach rolled. For a few seconds she sucked in cold air and let it out and stared at the ground between her boots, aware of the distant cry of a hawk somewhere far overhead, of the lapping of the fjord waters against the shoreline behind her, the whisper of the wind, cold and misty, smelling of evergreen, the constant creaking of the wreckage that had once been the plane. Somehow, she'd cut the back of her hand. Blood trailed between her fingers. She turned her hand over and studied her palm. Damp, slightly shiny, almost coagulated.

She flexed her hand. *Okay,* she thought. *I'm okay.*

With care, she rose to her height, brushed the dirt and debris off her jacket and jeans.

I can do this, she told herself.

Aside from a few superficial cuts and bruises and a throbbing bump on the side of her head, she was un-injured. Her trusty Timex had a compass feature, and she carried a map scribbled with arrows and instructions on how to get where she was going. The map—and the detailed instructions—had been provided by Medwyn, who'd been born in the Vildelund. She had enough food to last a few days. And she knew how to make a fire. Beneath her jacket was a thick wool sweater and beneath that, good-quality thermal under-wear. Her heavy-duty boots were broken in, and her socks were the best alpaca wool. She had a weapon and she knew how to use it if it came to that.

She may not have finished college, she might have trouble keeping a job, but life and death she could handle.

She *could* do this. She'd backpacked in the Sierras, done both the Appalachian and the Continental Divide trails. She would manage to find her way alone to the Village of the Mystics where Eric Greyfell—Med-wyn's son and hopefully the man to tell her the truth about how her brother Valbrand really died—was pur-ported to be living.

She would find Greyfell and she'd have the up-close and personal little talk she'd been itching to have with him. And when she got back to civilization, she'd find out who messed with the plane—and thus murdered poor Rutland. She'd see that the guilty were punished and that her father's men came for the dead guide, that his remains got the formal burial ceremony he deserved.

Look at it this way, she told herself, as she gauged the rugged upward sweep of craggy land before her. The plane crashing and Rutland dying was about the worst that could have happened. And guess what? It *had* happened.

The worst was over and she was still breathing.

Right then, something whizzed past her ear so close, it stirred her hair.

So much for the worst being over.

Brit went for her .45 as she dropped to one knee. She had the weapon half drawn when she heard a hiss and a *thwack*. Something punched her in the left shoulder.

An arrow! Wide-eyed in sickened disbelief, she stared along the shaft, following it to the head, which was buried in layers of fabric. Blood bloomed high on the front of her jacket. She could feel it spreading, warm and wet, under her sweater.

The good news? She felt no pain. Beyond the shock of impact, the wound itself was numb.

Also on the plus side, she wasn't dead yet.

She scanned the land before her, seeking her attacker—there. Stepping out from behind a big black boulder not fifty feet away. Some guy—way young, seventeen or eighteen, max. Long, tangled gold hair. Rigged out in rawhide leather with a mean-looking crossbow. The crossbow was pointed right at her. But she had her SIG out by then. With some fumbling, as her left hand didn't seem to be working too well, she levered the safety back—at which time, her left hand went limp. Very weird. But she was dealing with it.

Nice thing about the SIG 220. The kick wasn't all that bad. She could shoot it one-handed. She took aim.

It was a Mexican standoff—until everything started spinning.

Now it was her damn *right* hand. Something wrong with it, too. It had gone heavy. She couldn't hold it extended. It fell, nerveless, to her side, the pistol dropping to the rocks.

Well, okay. *Now* she was dead.

But just before the arrow took flight, as her body gave way and she began a strange, slow, nerveless slide to the ground, she heard a gunshot. Her too-young would-be assassin grunted and jerked back. The arrow meant to pierce her heart went wild.

And Brit was flat on the ground—drugged somehow. From the arrow in her shoulder? Must be. She wasn't out yet, not exactly, but hovering in some hazy, halfway place between waking and nothingness.

She lay on the rocks, the wind whistling overhead. She could see that hawk she'd heard before. It soared high up there, in the distant, cold blue yonder, dark wings spread against the sky.

Footsteps came crunching toward her across the rocks. A man was bending over her. An angular, arresting face. Deep-set, hypnotic gray-green eyes. She knew him from the pictures that sweet old Medwyn had made a special point of showing her.

He was Medwyn's only son, Eric Greyfell, the one she'd come to see.

And there. At Greyfell's side. Another. All in black. His face hidden behind a smooth black leather mask.

The things you see when you're probably dying…

And her eyes refused to stay open any longer. They drifted slowly shut.

There was silence.

Peace.

Oblivion.

There was a time of purest silence and velvet darkness.

Then came hot delirium. She burned within, her body ran with sweat.

And there were dreams.

In the dreams, she had visitors. Elli first. Elli was her middle sister. They were three, the sisters, fraternal triplets born within hours of one another: Liv then Elli then Brit.

"Oh, Brit." Elli wore her Viking wedding dress—and her most patient expression. She carried her wedding sword out before her, point down, jeweled hilt gleaming. She floated above the ground, surrounded by light as golden as her hair. "What have you gotten into now?"

"Ell, you look fabulous."

"You don't."

"Well, it's just…I'm so hot. Burning up…"

Elli made a *tsking* sound. "You should have gotten your degree at least, don't you think? Or maybe finished one of those novels you're always starting, before you went off and got yourself killed?"

"Not dead. Uh-uh. Not dead yet…"

"Didn't I warn you?" That was Liv, dressed for success in a cream-colored ensemble and those Mikimoto pearls that Granny Birgit had given her. Liv was bending over Brit, looking down, a scowl on her face, blue eyes narrowed, smooth blond hair falling forward against her cheeks. "Our dear father, His Majesty the king, has the whole palace bugged. Spies everywhere. How *can* you call him Dad? He as good as abandoned us, the daughters he didn't need...until both his sons were lost."

"He is what he is...."

"You should have kept your promise to Mom and come home with me in the first place. Then you wouldn't be here. Sweating and delirious. Dying."

"Hot. So hot..." Brit shut her eyes.

And when she opened them again, she could see her father. He seemed far away, standing behind his massive desk in his private audience chamber at the royal palace, Isenhalla. But at the same time he was there. With her. Looming over her, looking down at her. Firelight gleamed in his silver-shot dark hair and flashed off the ruby ring of state. Blood-red refractions danced everywhere. "Brit. Be strong."

"So hot..."

"Fight. In your veins runs the blood of kings. I have big plans for you. Don't you dare to die and disappoint me."

"No, Dad. I won't die. I swear I won't...."

But her father only shook his head sadly—and disappeared.

Her mother stood in his place, tall and beautiful and thoroughly exasperated. "What are you *doing,* Brit? What were you *thinking?*"

"Mom," she cried, reaching, crying out again when pain lanced through her shoulder. "Oh, Mommy, I'm so sorry...." But like the others, her mother had vanished.

Gentle hands guided her back to lie among the furs. An old woman with kind eyes bent close and whispered coaxingly, "It's all right. Rest. You're safe here."

And there were other voices, soft voices. They whispered of the poison that burned through her body, they murmured that now they could only wait and watch and keep her as comfortable as possible. They spoke to her soothingly. They bathed her sweating face with cool wet cloths.

And then, within the swirling, firelit twilight...

The one whose picture she carried with her, in her pack. The dead brother she'd never know.

Valbrand.

A hot bolt of fiercest joy shot through her. Not lost! Not dead, after all.

Oh, she had known it, though until this moment she hadn't quite dared to admit it even to herself.

Yet it had been there, against all odds, deep in her most secret heart. No one had really believed she would learn anything new when she said she would find the truth about what happened to him—well, okay, her father believed, at least a little. And Medwyn. After all, they had sent her here to find out what she could.

But no one else had any hope. Not her mother. Not her sisters. Not even Jorund Sorenson, the ally she'd cultivated at the National Investigative Bureau.

They all told her the truth was known already: Valbrand had died at sea.

She'd told herself they were probably right, that she only sought Eric Greyfell to understand better *how* her brother had died.

But still, she had *known*.

And she'd been right.

She tried to say his name. But words wouldn't come.

Valbrand. Tall and strong and so very alive. Standing right there, next to where she lay. He was dressed all in black, like the masked figure she'd seen in the heart of the fjord as she stared up, numb and fading, from the cold, rocky ground.

Had that been him, then—the masked one, in the fjord?

Valbrand was looking at Eric Greyfell, who stood beside him.

Eric warned her brother, "She sees you. She *knows* you. You shouldn't be here, not without the mask."

One of the soft-voiced women who tended her whispered, "She knows nothing. She's trapped in her world of fevered dreams...."

Her brother, still looking at Greyfell, smiled. His smile was rueful, sad and teasing all at once. "The littlest of my little sisters..."

Not so little, Brit thought, irritated. Just because she was the youngest by barely two hours didn't give anyone—even her long-lost and recently dead brother—the right to call her "little."

She tried to tell him that, but again the words would not take form. Valbrand was still looking at Eric, still smiling fondly. "Your bride," he said. The two words echoed. They bounced off the rough wooden walls.

Your bride, your bride, your bride, your bride...

Greyfell's expression gave away nothing. "If she lives."

"She'll live," said Valbrand. "Thor and Freyja protect her equally. Hers is the thunder, hers is love.'' He chuckled. ''And war...''

And then he looked directly at her. She saw that something terrible had happened to the left side of his face. It was crisscrossed and puckered with ridges of white scar tissue, the flesh between ruined, ranging from angry red to deep purple. What could do such a thing to a man?

Acid? A blowtorch?

She cried out in pity and despair.

The gentle hands caught her, guiding her down. The soft voices soothed her. ''Rest now, you're safe....''

Chapter Two

Slowly, the burning heat faded. The dreams receded.

Brit woke weak and exhausted. She found herself in a large wooden room, bare rafters overhead. The windows were small and set high up. Thin daylight bled in through them. Very carefully she turned her head.

She saw a big, round-bodied stove in the center of the room, the chimney rising through the rafters above. And a pair of long, plain benches on either side of a plank table made of whitish wood—a deal table, she would have bet. Deal was the pale wood that came from the Norway spruce. There were oil lamps set in sconces on the walls. She lay on a bench-like bed built into one wall. Her blankets? A nest of furs. Someone had dressed her in a soft cotton nightgown.

There was a woman—a slim, straight-backed

woman with white hair. She wore a thick, coarsely woven ankle-length tan dress and good-quality rough-terrain lace-up boots. She sat on a high stool at the far end of the room, her back to Brit. She was working at something that looked as if it might be an old-fashioned loom.

Brit licked her dry, cracked lips. Was this real? Was this actually happening? Or was it just another of her endless, swirling dreams?

She sat up. Her shoulder throbbed, her stomach lurched and her head spun, but she didn't lie back down. "Valbrand?" she managed to croak out through her parched throat. "Eric Greyfell...?"

The woman rose and came to her. "There, there. It's all right. You're safe."

She remembered that kind, wrinkled face, those loving eyes. "I...I know you. You took care of me."

"You've been very ill," the woman said as she guided Brit back down and tucked the furs around her again. "We feared we'd lose you. But you're strong. You will recover."

It came back to her then: the Skyhawk, the forced landing, the death of her guide. "Rutland...my guide?" Maybe that part—the part where she saw the guide dead—was only another of the fever dreams.

The kind-faced old woman shook her head. "What can be done has been done."

"But I..."

The woman had already turned away. She went to the stove, dipped up liquid from an iron pot with a wooden cup. Cup in hand, she returned to Brit's side. "Your guide's body was sent to his family in the valley just south of this one."

So. That part was real. Twin tears dribbled down the sides of her face. "My fault…"

"No. What fate has decreed, no mere mortal can alter."

"It wasn't fate, it was my own arrogance, my own certainty that I could—"

"Here." The woman bent close again, lifted Brit's head and put the cup to her lips. "Drink. This will soothe you."

"But I—"

"Drink."

Brit lacked the energy to argue further. She drank. The warm, sweet liquid felt good sliding down her dry throat.

"There," said the woman. She set the empty cup on the floor. It must have tipped. Brit heard it roll beneath the wooden ledge that served as her bed. The woman ignored it long enough to carefully smooth Brit's furs again. "Rest now." She dropped out of sight as she got down to reach under the bed. In a moment, with a weary little grunt, she was on her feet, cup in hand. She started to turn.

"Wait…" The old woman faced her again, one gray brow arched. "My brother. I want to see him."

The woman shook her head. "Princess, you know that your brothers are gone."

"Kylan, yes." Kylan was the second born. He had died years and years ago, when he was only a child. "But not Valbrand. I saw him. In this room, while I was so sick. His face, the left side, it was…badly scarred."

There was a short silence. The fire crackled in the

stove. Then the woman said, "A dream, that's all. A dream brought on by your fever."

"No, he was here. He—"

"Prince Valbrand is dead, Your Highness. Lost to us. Surely you knew. He was taken by the mother sea a year ago this past July." The woman spoke so tenderly, with such sincere sympathy.

Brit opened her mouth to argue further, but then the woman leaned close again. A silver medallion dangled from her neck. It must have swung free of her dress when she bent for the cup. Brit couldn't resist reaching out and touching it. It spun a little on its chain, catching the firelight. The sight made Brit smile.

The woman smiled, too, the web of wrinkles in her face etching all the deeper. "My marriage medallion."

Marriage? Brit frowned. And then she sighed. "I have one, too." Brit pressed the place where her medallion lay beneath the nightgown, warm against her breast. "From Medwyn, my father's grand counselor. But mine's only for luck."

"Ah," said the woman, a strange and too-knowing expression on her wise, very lived-in face. "Sleep now."

Brit did feel tired. But she had so many questions. "Where am I?"

"You are where you wished to be, among the ones they call the Mystics."

"How long have I been…sick?"

"This is the fourth day."

Her plane had gone down on Monday. "Thursday? It's Thursday?"

"Yes."

"How did I—?"

"Eric found you. He brought you to us."

Hope bloomed, a small, bright flame, within her. "Greyfell found me—in Drakveden Fjord?"

"That's right."

"But then, it must be true." The woman frowned down at her, clearly puzzled. "I saw him—Eric Greyfell—in Drakveden Fjord, where I crashed the Skyhawk. Valbrand was with him, I swear he was. Wearing a black mask. And there was this guy with a crossbow..." She laid her hand over the thick bandage on her shoulder. "Someone shot him before he could—"

"Hush." The woman's warm wrinkled hand stroked her brow. "No more questions now. Sleep."

"My father. My mother and my sisters...they'll be so worried...."

"Word has been sent to the king that you are safe with us."

The questions spun in her brain. She needed the answers. But the woman was right. There were too many to ask right now. She could barely keep her eyes open.

"Sleep," the woman whispered. Something about her was so familiar.

"Please...your name?"

"I'm Asta. Medwyn's sister. Eric's aunt."

So, Brit thought. Medwyn's sister. She should have known, of course. Medwyn had told her of Asta, and she could see the resemblance around the eyes and in the shape of the mouth. "Asta." It was pronounced with the *As* like twin sighs: Ahstah. "It's a pretty name."

"Thank you, Your Highness. Now sleep."

"Yes. All right. I will. Sleep..."

*   *   *

Brit heard the playful giggle of a child. She opened her eyes in time to watch a mop of shiny blond curls disappear over the side of the sleeping bench.

A few seconds later the curls popped up again, along with a pair of china-blue eyes and a cute little turned-up nose. The eyes widened. "Oops." The small face popped out of sight again. There was more giggling below.

Brit grinned and whispered in a dry croak, "I see you."

More giggles. And then the little head rose into view once more. The rosebud mouth widened in a shy smile. The child raised a thumb and pointed it at her tiny chest. "Mist."

"Hello, Mist. I'm Brit."

"Bwit." The child called Mist beamed with pleasure. "Pwincess Bwit."

"Just Brit will do."

"Just Bwit. Bwit, Bwit, Bwit…"

"Mist," Asta chided from over by the stove where she sat with two younger women, a circle of children playing some sort of game with sticks and a tiny red ball at their feet. "Leave Her Highness to sleep."

"It's all right." Brit winked at the child and pulled herself to a sitting position, wincing at the sharp twinge from the wound in her shoulder. Sunlight slanted in the high slits of the windows. Late morning, Brit thought. Or possibly early afternoon. She let her head fall forward to stretch her stiff neck, and her tangled hair fell over her eyes. She speared her fingers in it to shove it back.

Ugh. A serious shampooing and a little intimate contact with a decent conditioner would do wonders about now. Not to mention a long, hot bath. She heard a growling sound—her stomach. She could eat half a polar bear, or whatever they were serving here in the Vildelund. But first, water. A tall, cool, glorious glass of it.

However, she hesitated to throw back the furs and go looking for a drink in her thin borrowed nightgown with all these strange women and children in the room. "I wonder, could I have some water?"

"Of course." Asta set aside her sewing and went to the big wooden counter against one wall. The sink was there, complete with an ancient-looking pump faucet. Asta pumped clear water into a tall cup and carried it to Brit.

She drank. It was absolute heaven going down.

From her seat on the floor, Mist giggled some more. "Bwit fuhsty." *Fuhsty,* Brit figure out, had to mean thirsty.

Brit swallowed the last of it. "Was I ever. Thanks." She handed Asta back the empty cup. The women by the fire were watching her. She gave them a nod. "I seem to remember you two being here while I was sick…"

"I forget myself," said Asta. "Your Highness, my daughters-in-law, Sif and Sigrid. Mist, whom you've met, is Sif's youngest." She named off the other children. Two were Sigrid's and two, Sif's.

"Great to meet you all." Brit turned to Asta again. "And now…what's for dinner?"

Asta's smile was wide and pleased. "Your health improves."

"It certainly does."

"Bah-wee soup," announced Mist.

"That's barley," Asta explained.

Brit wrinkled her nose. "I was thinking more along the lines of steak and eggs and hash browns."

"Your stomach isn't ready for solid food yet."

Brit sighed. "Barley soup it is." She gave Asta a big smile. "And would you go and tell my brother I'd like to see him now, please?"

It seemed, for a moment, as if the room was too quiet. Then Asta spoke carefully. "We talked of this earlier. Perhaps you've forgotten. Your brother is—"

Brit waved a hand. "Never mind. I remember. So, if my brother's not available, could you track down your nephew, Eric, please? It's imperative that I speak with him."

Sif and Sigrid shared a look. Asta suggested, "Eat first. See how you feel."

Asta dished up a big bowl of broth with barley and cut a thick slice from a loaf of dark bread. She carried it over to Brit on a wooden tray.

By the time she'd eaten half the soup and taken a bite of the bread, Brit was ready to call it quits on the food front. "I guess I sort of miscalculated how much I could eat." Also, she was tired again. This convalescing thing was *so* inconvenient. She handed Asta the bowl. "Thank you."

"You are most welcome, Your High—"

"I wonder, could we dispense with the 'Your Highness' routine?"

Asta looked pleased. "I would be honored."

"It's Brit, then, all right?"

"Yes. Brit. Good enough."

"Now, if you could just get me my clothes and—"

Asta was gently pushing her down. "All that can wait. Rest, now. You're not ready to get out of bed."

Brit found she tended to agree with Asta. So annoying. She felt tired to the bone. She didn't have the energy to get dressed—let alone to deal with Eric Greyfell. She gave Asta a rueful smile. "Sorry, but there's one thing that *can't* wait."

Asta brought her a pair of clogs and wrapped a shawl around her shoulders as the women by the fire continued with their needlework and the group of children played their game and little Mist sat on the floor near Brit's sleeping bench, sucking her thumb and watching wide-eyed.

It was hard work, even leaning on Asta, to get all the way to the door and out into the crisp afternoon beyond. The thin sunlight, after the days inside, seemed blinding. Brit hardly had the energy to glance at the village around her—more long wooden houses, all grouped together along a single dirt street. There were pastures and paddocks behind the houses. Beyond the pastures, a thick forest of spruce flowed up the surrounding hills.

Asta noted her interest in the village houses. "Here we live in the old Norse way. In traditional longhouses—long, one-room dwellings where we eat, sleep, work and gather with our friends and family."

Each house had a small garden to one side of it. The pastureland beyond the gardens was dotted with karavik and sturdy, long-haired white Gullandrian horses. According to the map Medwyn had drawn for her, Drakveden Fjord wasn't far to the north. If she followed the fjord west, she should come to the site where her Skyhawk had gone down.

Not that she had the slightest inclination to go looking for it now. But someday soon. When the annoying weakness left over from her illness had passed.

At the end of the house, they reached a wooden lean-to. It had a sliver of moon carved into the top of the door. Just like in the old days in America, Brit thought. Was the moon on the door the international symbol for outhouse? She grinned to herself.

"Something humorous?" Asta wondered.

"Nothing important. And I don't think I'm going to ask how you handled this while I was so sick."

"We managed," Asta replied with her usual sunny smile. "I'll be right here when you're done."

Brit went in and shut the door. When she came out, Asta was waiting, as promised.

Brit forced a smile. "You are my hero, Asta, I hope you know it."

"I am honored to be of service."

"I have to ask, though I know it's going to make me sound like your classic ugly American—don't you ever think about putting in a bathroom, maybe adding electricity?"

Asta shrugged. "Here we live simply. It's a hard life, yes. But that is our way. We believe the simple life builds strong character and a clear mind—now come. Let's get you back to bed." Asta offered her shoulder. Brit accepted it gratefully. Slowly they shuffled back inside, where Asta helped her to get comfortable and brought her warm water from the stove and a soft cloth to wash her hands and rinse her face.

Brit was already half asleep again when Asta began checking the dressing on her bandage.

"Asta?"

"Hmm?"

"About my brother…"

"Shh. Sleep."

"Sweep, sweep, sweep," chanted Mist, over by the fire now with the other children.

Brit gave in and did as she was told.

The next time she woke, Eric Greyfell was sitting in a chair about two feet from her nest of furs.

She blinked, then muttered, "It's about time you showed up."

He nodded, one regal dip of his head. "My aunt informed me that you wished to speak with me." And then he just sat there, looking at her.

They were alone. The high windows were dark and the lamps were lit. "Where is Asta?"

"My aunt, as you may have deduced, is something of a healer. Her skills are needed elsewhere tonight."

It occurred to Brit that she'd met Asta's daughters-in-law and grandchildren. But she'd never seen a husband. "Your uncle?"

"He died several years ago."

She had assumed as much. "I'm sorry to hear it."

He shrugged. "We live, we die. That is the way of things. For my uncle's death, the time of mourning is long past."

"I see. Well, a good thing, right—I mean, that grief passes?" Sheesh. Talk about inane chatter. She was filling in time as she worked her way around to what was really on her mind: Valbrand.

And the little detail no one seemed to want to talk about—the fact that he wasn't dead, after all.

Greyfell said nothing. The fire crackled in the stove and Brit stared at Medwyn's son, wondering how best to get him to admit that her brother was alive—and to convince him that he should bring Valbrand to her. Now.

As she debated how to begin, he watched her. She found his hooded gaze unnerving. "Why do you look at me like that?"

"Like what, precisely?"

She wished she hadn't asked. "Never mind."

He stood and came closer, until he loomed over her, his deep-set eyes lost in the shadows beneath the shelf of his brow. She stared up at those shadowed eyes and wished he hadn't come so near. She felt like a total wimp, lying there in somebody else's nightgown, weak and shaky and flat on her back.

She sat up—fast enough that her head spun and pain sliced through her shoulder. "Listen."

"Yes?"

His shoulder-length ash-brown hair had a slight curl to it. He wore it loose, though it seemed it had been tied back—in the fjord and that time he stood over her when she was so sick. Now it looked just-combed, smooth and shiny. He smelled of the outdoors, fresh and piney and cool. She didn't want to think about what *she* smelled like. She clutched the furs close to her breast, as if they might protect her from his probing eyes. "Look. I just wanted to talk to you about…well, I mean, my brother…" She waited. Maybe he'd give it up, tell her the truth that everyone kept denying. Maybe he would see in her eyes how badly she needed confirmation that Valbrand lived.

Maybe he would realize that she could be trusted.

But it wasn't happening. He said nothing. She let out a low groan of frustration. "Can we skip the lies and evasions, please? Will you just let me speak with my brother?"

His mouth softened. He lifted his head a fraction, and the lamplight melted the shadows that hid his eyes.

Kind. His eyes were kind. They gleamed with sympathy. She hated that—his sympathy. It made her doubt what she knew in her heart. And it made her soften toward him. She didn't need softening. She was weak enough already.

He spoke so gently, each word uttered with great care. "You must accept that your brother is dead."

"No."

"Yes."

Brit clutched the furs tighter and wished she didn't feel so tired. She wanted to keep after him, to break him down, to get him to admit what they both knew was true. But how?

Her mind felt thick and slow. Weariness dragged at her. All he had to do was stay kind and steady—and keep on with the denials. Eventually she would have to give up and go back to sleep.

She spoke softly, pleadingly, though it galled her to do it. "I saw him. In the fjord, with you, I'm sure of it, though then he was wearing a mask—but here, when I was sick, I saw his face. Please stop lying. Please stop implying that I was too sick and confused to know what I saw. Please admit—"

"I cannot admit what never happened." His deep, rich voice was weighted with just the right measure of regret. He seemed so sincere. She could almost begin to believe he spoke the truth. And to doubt what her eyes had seen...

"He *was* here. I know it."

Gently, so regretfully, he shook his head.

She swallowed. Her mouth was so dry.

And this was a subject better pursued when she was stronger. "I wonder. Would you mind getting me some water?"

"It would be my pleasure."

He went to the sink. While he pumped the water she tried to come up with some new approach, some brilliant line of questioning that would make him open up to her. She drew a complete blank.

And he was back with a full cup. "Do you need help?"

"Thanks. I can manage." She held out her hand, pleased to see that it hardly shook at all. He passed her the cup. She drank long and deep, sighing when she finished.

He was watching, the slightest of smiles tipping the corners of his mouth. "Good?"

"Wonderful."

"More?"

"I would appreciate it." She held out the cup. Their fingers brushed as he took it from her. It seemed, for some reason, a far too intimate contact. He went to the sink again and she watched him go. He wore heavy tan trousers, mountain boots and an oatmeal-colored thermal shirt. He had a great butt. He also carried himself proudly—like the king everyone thought he might someday be now they all believed that Valbrand was gone.

In Gullandria, succession was never assured. All male jarl, or nobles, were princes. Any prince might put himself forward as a candidate for king when the current king could no longer rule and the jarl gathered in the Grand Assembly for the election ceremony known as the kingmaking.

Since childhood, Eric had been groomed, not for the throne, but to one day take his father's place as grand counselor. It had been Valbrand, everyone felt certain, who would win the throne. King Osrik was a respected and effective ruler. The country had prospered during his reign. And the people loved Valbrand. That made him the logical next choice.

But then Valbrand went to sea and didn't come back. And Osrik and Medwyn turned their sights to Eric as the one to claim the crown when the time came. The two had schemed shamelessly. Eric, they decided, should marry one of Osrik's estranged daughters....

The potential king in question had reached the sink. He stood with his back to her, broad-shouldered, narrow-hipped, regal even from the rear, pumping water into her cup.

Brit allowed herself a wide grin.

Her father and Medwyn's schemes kept backfiring. Elli had fallen in love with the man they'd sent to kidnap her. And on Elli's wedding night, Liv had dallied with the notorious Prince Finn Danelaw. She'd become pregnant as a result. And Eric? After months spent in search of the truth about Valbrand's supposed death, Eric had come here, to the Vildelund. He'd resisted his father's repeated requests that he return to the palace and begin preparing for his future as king.

Yes, Brit knew that her father and Medwyn considered her next in line to be Eric's bride. But she'd made it clear to them that romance wasn't on her agenda. She was after the truth about Valbrand. Period.

King Osrik and Medwyn had said they accepted that. And if they didn't, so what? Her father and his grand counselor could plot and plan to their heart's content. She had a goal. Marrying Eric Greyfell wasn't it.

"Brit?"

She blinked. Eric was standing right over her, holding the full cup. "Oh, uh, sorry. Just woolgathering." He wore an expectant look. Maybe he didn't get her meaning. "Woolgathering is an expression. It means—"

"Purposeless thinking." Those deep-set eyes gleamed. "Aimless reverie. The word is derived from the actual process of woolgathering, which entails wandering the countryside, gathering up bits of wool from bushes that karavik—sheep—have brushed up against."

"Very good."

"And where, exactly, did your woolgathering take you?"

She took the cup again and sipped. She was stalling. She really didn't feel up to going into it—especially since it would only lead to the part about how their fathers hoped they'd hook up. "It's not important."

"Somehow I don't believe you."

"Then we're even, aren't we?" She drank the last and handed back the empty cup. "You know what?

I'm really tired. I appreciate your coming and talking to me.'' She stretched out and pulled up the furs. ''You don't have to stay until your aunt gets back. I'll be fine, I promise.'' She snuggled down deeper and shut her eyes. Sleep came almost instantly.

Eric stood over Valbrand's youngest sister and watched her face soften as she drifted into the land of dreams. She had great courage. She'd sought him out in the wild land of his birth, alone but for a single guide to show her the way. She'd lived through the crash that had killed her guide, emerging unaided from the wreckage of her plane, armed and ready to face whatever waited outside. She possessed spirit and stamina—few survived a hit from a renegade's poisoned arrow. And he liked her fine, quick mind.

Her eyes had dark smudges beneath them. A limp coil of lank blond hair lay across her cheek. He dared, very gently, to smooth it back, careful of the still-livid bruise at her temple.

She sighed, a tiny smile curving her cracked, dry lips. He felt the corners of his own mouth lifting in instinctive response.

He supposed he was willing to admit it now. His father had chosen well.

Chapter Three

It was much later when Brit woke again. The lamps were out, though night still ruled beyond the high-set windows. The fire had burned low. It cast a muted glow out the stove door window, spilling soft gold light across the table a few feet away. Where Brit lay, in the far corner, the shadows were thickest.

She sat up. Wow. Her head didn't spin and her shoulder throbbed only dully.

There were three other wide, wall-mounted benches like the one where she slept. One of them—down the wall past another bed, sharp right, then halfway down the next wall—was occupied. And not by the kindly old woman who had brought her back from near death.

Eric lay with his furs to his waist, his eyes shut, face turned toward the center of the room, one arm to his side, the other across his chest.

So had he been sleeping there last night, and the night before? She really hadn't noticed. She'd been far too busy sweating and hallucinating. Strange, to think of him, living here in Asta's longhouse, sleeping in the same room with her and her not even knowing it.

Moonlight from the window across the room slanted down on him, making shadows and silver of the strong planes and angles of his face, defining more sharply the sculpted perfection of his lean, bare chest and hard arms.

The guy really was gorgeous.

And she really, really had to pee.

She figured by now she was strong enough to handle at least that problem on her own. Easing back the furs, she swung her feet over the edge. The clogs were right there, toes peeking out beneath the bench—bless you, Asta.

Brit slid her feet into them. Then, slowly, she stood. Ta-da! Upright and okay about it. So far, so good.

She grabbed one of the furs from her bed and wrapped herself up in it. And then, as quietly as she could, she started for the door.

Ever try to tiptoe in clogs?

She got about four steps when Eric spoke from behind her. "What are you doing out of bed?"

She sighed. "Sorry. Didn't mean to wake you. I just have to make a quick trip outside." She was pointed toward the door and she stayed that way. She had a feeling he was naked under the furs and she also knew that he was going to insist on getting up and helping her out to the lean-to. If the rest of him looked half as good as what she'd already seen...

Down, girl. Don't go there.

"I'll go with you," he said.

Surprise, surprise. "Make it quick, okay? The situation is getting urgent." She shuffled forward. He must have had his pants nearby, because she only got a few steps before he was taking her elbow. He wore fur-lined moccasin-style slippers over bare feet, the tan trousers he'd worn earlier and no shirt. She cast a meaningful glance at his hard, bare chest. "I'll bet it's nippy out there."

He shrugged, pulled open the door and ushered her out into the starry, cold night. Ten steps and they were at the lean-to.

"Be right out." She hustled in and shut the door.

Boy, was she grateful she wasn't wearing any panties. It was a near thing, but she sat down in time. And after the initial relief, she worried about what women always worry about when they're performing a private function and some guy is standing right outside.

She was sure he could hear everything.

Life in the Mystic village was a little *too* simple for her tastes. Give her insulated walls. And a real toilet that flushed, with a seat that didn't leave slivers in inconvenient places. And a bedroom door to shut when she went to sleep at night, for crying out loud.

When she opened the door again, he was waiting right there, those lean, strong arms crossed over the goose bumps on his beautiful smooth chest. "Ready?" He held out an arm for her.

"I can make it on my own, I think."

He shrugged and fell in behind her.

Inside, she turned for the sink. He followed. Her irritation level rose. Okay, she'd been seriously sick.

But she was well enough now to walk to the sink unattended.

But then he said, "Here," and manned the pump. She rinsed her hands and couldn't resist splashing a little icy water on her face, sipping up a mouthful or two. When she was done, he handed her a towel. She wiped her face. He bent and picked up the fur that had dropped to the rough wooden floor while she reveled in the feel of the water against her cheeks. He gestured toward her sleeping bench. "Back to bed."

It sounded like a great idea. She clomped over, left the heavy clogs where she'd found them and stretched out. He settled the fur over her. "Sleep now."

She couldn't help smiling. "Your aunt's always saying that."

"It's good advice. You've been very ill."

"Is she still at the neighbor's?"

He nodded. "It doesn't look good. A heart attack, we think. The man is young, too. Barely forty."

"Shouldn't he be in a hospital?"

"The man's a true Mystic. No hospitals for him."

"But if he dies—"

His eyes gleamed down at her through the shadows. "It's a choice, to make a life here. With few conveniences. No phones, poor access to emergency care. Most who live here embrace the realities of this place."

They were both whispering. It was nice—companionable. A quiet little chat in the midnight darkness. "Why?"

"They find peace here. And real meaning to their lives."

She smiled, thinking again of what Asta had told

her. A simple life, one that made for strong character and a clear mind. "I was surprised tonight, when I woke up and you were sleeping right over there."

"I live here, in my aunt's house, when I'm staying at the village."

She let a second or two elapse before she asked, "And where does my brother live?"

He didn't answer right away. She had a lovely, rising feeling. He would tell her the truth. And then she would keep after him until he agreed to take her to wherever Valbrand was staying.

But then he said softly, "Your brother lies forever sleeping—at the bottom of the sea."

She bit her lower lip to stop its sudden trembling. "That was cruel."

"The truth is often cruel."

She looked him dead in the eyes. "But it's not the truth. It's a lie. I saw him. You know I did. You were right beside him, standing almost where you're standing now. You said, 'She sees you. She *knows* you.'"

"In your dream."

"It wasn't a dream."

He was already turning away. "Good night, Brit."

Good night, Brit. Damn him, he so easily called her by her first name. Everyone else fell all over themselves Your-Highnessing her to death. But Eric Greyfell had presumed to address her with familiarity from the first.

And come to think of it, why did it bug her so much that he did? As a rule, since she'd come to Gullandria, she was constantly asking people to please just call her Brit.

She heard faint rustlings over by his furs. He would be taking off his trousers, slipping into bed....

"Eric?"

"Yes?" He sounded wary.

And well he should. "You do have some way, don't you, of contacting my father—and yours?"

"There is radio contact, yes. It can be undependable, but eventually we get through."

"Is that how you got hold of my father to tell him what had happened to me?"

"That's right."

"So why didn't he send a helicopter to take me out of here and get me to a hospital?"

He was silent for several seconds. The remains of a log popped in the grate, the sound jarring in the quiet room.

Getting impatient, she prompted, "Eric?"

"Is that what you would have wanted, to be airlifted out of here, had you been able to make the decision for yourself?"

She considered for a moment, then admitted, "No."

"Then it was done as you would have wished."

"But who decided that I would stay here, at your aunt's village, instead of going to a hospital? My brother?"

Did he chuckle then, very low? She thought he might have. "That would have been difficult for him, as he is dead."

She scowled at the ceiling. "This radio—where is it?"

"Here, in the village."

"So. You brought me here, and then you contacted my father..."

"Yes."

"And my father decided that I would stay?"

"Your father. And mine. Your father knows you—better than you might think."

"And *your* father?"

"Some say he has a way of seeing the secrets that lie in the hearts and minds of others. He understood that you were set on a certain course, that if they took you away, you would only return."

"But if I had died…"

"My father also felt certain you were meant to survive. And to grow strong again. There's an old Norse saying…"

As if she hadn't heard it a hundred times already. "'The length of my life and the day of my death were fated long ago.'" He did chuckle then, loud enough that there was no mistaking the sound. She couldn't stop herself from asking, "And you—how did you feel about having to drag an almost-dead woman out of Drakveden Fjord and all the way to your aunt's village?"

"It was a difficult journey over rough country. It took most of a day and into the night. I felt certain, for a time at least, that you wouldn't survive."

"And when my father and your father decided I would stay?"

"I had my doubts it was the right decision—but now, here you are. Alive. Growing stronger. I see that I was wrong to doubt."

"You certainly were. And, Eric?"

"Yes?"

"Your father was right. My course is set. I'm not

going away until I speak with my brother face-to-face.''

There was silence.

Which was okay with Brit. Right then there was nothing more to say.

When Brit woke to daylight, Eric was gone. Asta lay beneath the furs on the bed just down the hall.

Quietly, wanting to let the old woman sleep, Brit got up and tiptoed to the sink. She washed her hands and took a long drink and then went back to bed. She was thinking that maybe she might sleep some more.

Not. Her stomach kept growling. And she wanted a bath. At the same time she didn't really know how to go about getting food or getting clean without Asta's help.

For fifteen minutes or so, Brit lay staring at the rafters, telling herself to ignore her growling stomach and go back to sleep. About then, quietly, the door opened. Eric. He entered on silent feet. His hair was wet, his face freshly shaven. He carried what looked like yesterday's clothing and a small leather case: shaving supplies? He went to his bed and stashed everything beneath it.

She sat up. He glanced her way and she signaled him over. When he reached her and she smelled soap and water on him, she whispered, ''I know you've had a bath. Who do I have to kill to get one myself?''

He crouched to drag her pack out from under her sleeping bench. ''Get what you need,'' he instructed low, pulling her jacket out, too. She saw that the arrow hole had been neatly mended and the blood stain treated. Blood is so stubborn, though. The stain was faint, but still here. "Come," he said. "I'll show you the way."

The village bathhouse—divided in two; one side for the women, the other for the men—was several doors down from Asta's. They had actual indoor plumbing and a huge, propane-burning water heater behind the building, Eric told her. And towels, stacks of them, on shelves along one wall. There were two other women inside, just finishing up. They greeted Brit politely and went on their way.

Brit took off her coat and her nightgown and debated over the large bandage that covered the wound on her shoulder. She decided to leave it, let it get wet, and then figure out what to do about changing it when she got back to the longhouse. She showered, washed her hair and brushed her teeth. Then she put on clean clothes and emerged to find Eric waiting outside for her.

She hadn't expected him to do that. "You didn't have to stay. I can manage the walk back on my own."

"Here," he said, taking her nightgown from over her arm. "That, too." He indicated her vanity pack.

"No, it's all right. Really. I can—"

He waved away her objections, his hand out, waiting for her to give him the pack. With a sigh, she did. He offered her his arm.

Oh, why not? She slipped her hand into the crook of his elbow and they started off.

She clomped along the hard-packed dirt street beside him, shivering a little, eager to get back to the longhouse, to dry her hair by the fire and do something about her uncomfortable soggy bandage—and most important, to find a way to get him to be straight with her.

What, exactly, was he up to here? He refused to stop lying and take her to her brother—a fact that she realized might very well be because Valbrand wanted it that way.

But it wasn't only the big lie he kept telling.

It was also that he was just…such a hottie. And she kept getting the feeling that he was very subtly coming on to her—which was something she *so* didn't need at this point in her life. It would only muck up her focus, add complications she wasn't up to dealing with.

Plus, if he really *was* coming on to her—which, face it, could very well be nothing more than a sort of contrary wishful thinking on her part—why? Because their fathers wanted them to get married and settle down to rule the country? Doubtful. Because she was so incredibly sexy and alluring, with a hole in her shoulder and bruises on her bruises, no makeup and, until about fifteen minutes ago, very dirty hair and serious morning breath? Not.

The deal was, she couldn't figure him out. And until she did, she was going to be wary of him. She didn't trust him. And yet…

It *had* been nice of him to wait. And his arm was warm and strong and steady, his body heat comforting.

They passed a few people as they made their way to Asta's house. A man carrying firewood. A woman with a baby in a papoose-like contraption on her back. Eric nodded, and the villagers nodded back, sparing smiles for Brit, along with murmured Your Highnesses and expressions of pleasure at her improving health.

In the longhouse Asta still slept—a lump beneath the furs, curled up and turned to the wall.

Brit whispered to Eric. "The man she was nursing?"

"It appears he'll survive, after all."

She smiled at the good news as she took off her coat—easing it carefully over her bad shoulder—and hung it on one of the wooden pegs near the door. The clogs made too much noise, so she slipped them off and set them with Asta's pair, beneath the coatrack. In her heavy socks, she padded to her sleeping bench, where she stowed the rest of her things. When she turned back toward the center of the room, Eric was watching her, his gaze tracking to where the water from her soaked bandage was seeping through her shirt. She wondered what else he was looking at. She hadn't taken a bra to the bathhouse. Right now, with her shoulder so stiff, it would have hurt like hell to get into one. And she'd only be taking it off again, anyway. Because as soon as she rebandaged her wound and ate something, her hair should be dry enough that she could climb back into bed.

"Let me change that." His voice was so soft, the verbal equivalent of a caress.

They gazed at each other. It was another of those edgy, what-is-really-happening-here? moments. She blinked and started to tell him no.

But the bandage had to be changed. Asta was asleep. Brit would probably make a mess of it if she tried to do it herself—and, hey, at least her thermal shirt had a zipper front. She should be able to get it out of his way and still keep the crucial parts covered.

"All right, I'd appreciate it—just hold on a minute.'' She turned for her pack beneath her bed. In a side pocket she had three precious bags of peanut M&Ms. She took one out, opened it and got herself a nice, fat blue one. She held out the bag to Eric. Looking puzzled, he shook his head. She put it away.

When she approached the table again, he asked, "What is that?"

She held up the blue candy. ''M&M. Peanut. I love them.''

For that she got a lifted eyebrow. ''And you must have one...now?''

''I find them soothing—and don't worry. It's not drugs or anything. Just sugar and chocolate and a peanut at the center.'' He still had that I-don't-get-it look. So all right, she was nervous, okay? There was something way too intimate about him tending her wound. ''Could we just...do this?'' She stuck the candy in her mouth.

''As you wish.'' He gestured for her to sit at the table. Then he turned toward the sink area—presumably to get fresh bandages and tape.

Brit seized the moment, perching with her back to him at the end of one of the two long benches, and swiftly unzipping her shirt. She heard the slight creak of the sink pump. He must be washing his hands. She pulled the shirt down her left arm—too roughly, hurt like a mother—and got into trouble trying to reinsert the slide into the stopper thingy.

He was finished at the sink. She heard him approach behind her, moving quietly, halting at her back.

''Just a minute,'' she muttered, already chewing her only half-sucked M&M, hunched over the zipper, feeling exposed and ridiculous and still battling to get the damn thing to hook.

"No hurry."

She felt her face flaming as she continued to struggle, the pain an extra irritant as her injured shoulder complained at the tension. At last she got it in. With a sigh of embarrassed relief, she zipped until she had her breasts covered, the left arm of the shirt hanging beneath her own arm.

She turned to him, certain she would find him smirking or quelling a smarmy chuckle. He wasn't, on either count. He was, however, staring at her chest. He shifted his gaze up to meet her eyes—and she understood.

He'd been looking at her medallion.

She might so easily have lifted it on its chain and mentioned that his father had given it to her. But she didn't. Somehow, the idea of drawing attention to it seemed unwise, even dangerous. "Okay. Do it."

He set his equipment on the table: a roll of gauze, tape, scissors and a tube of ointment. Then he returned to the sink, where he grabbed a cloth from a shelf and filled a wooden bowl halfway with water. At the stove he took the steaming kettle and poured hot water to mix with the cold in the bowl. He returned to her, setting the bowl down, dropping the cloth into it.

He went to work. Once again, with him so near, she became way too aware of the fresh, outdoorsy smell of him. His hands were gentle—quick and skilled. She found herself wondering how many wounds he'd bandaged.

"It's just as well you got it wet," he whispered. "It's not sticking."

She averted her eyes through most of the process, but when he had the soggy bandage off, she looked down at the damage. It wasn't pretty—ragged and red, still draining a little. There was going to be a scar, for sure. "I guess I won't be going strapless to the ball."

He gently cleaned the wound with the warm, damp cloth. "Wear your scars proudly. They speak of what you have faced—and what you have survived."

She looked at him then. Straight on. There were perhaps four inches between his mouth and hers. And his mouth was…so soft looking. Four inches. No distance at all. The slightest forward movement on her part and she would be kissing him.

Oh, now, why did she have to go and think of kisses? She pointedly shifted her gaze to a spot beyond his shoulder.

He went on with his work, finished swabbing the wound with the warm cloth, applied the ointment, which soothed the soreness and gave off a faint scent of cloves.

Finally, he taped on the fresh bandage. "There," he said, stepping back.

Her stomach growled. Loudly.

That mouth she'd almost found herself kissing curved up at the corners. "Oatmeal?"

"Please."

The heavy earthenware bowls waited in plain sight on open shelves. She set the table, doing her best to keep clatter to a minimum as he, equally quietly, fixed the food. They even had milk, which he removed from a small cellar under the floor. There was honey for sweetening. And a lovely tea that tasted of cinnamon—a tea almost good enough to make up for the lack of her usual four cups of morning coffee, strong and black.

She was tired again by the time the meal was over. She helped him clear off, and then he took the single-barreled shotgun from the rack above the door and a pack from under his sleeping bench and left.

Miraculously, Asta hadn't stirred through the changing of the bandage or the meal preparations. Brit plodded to her own furs and stretched out. She was clean and her stomach was full. Life, at the moment, was good.

She was asleep within minutes.

Brit woke again in the afternoon. Asta was up, surrounded by her grandchildren, her daughters-in-law sitting with her near the fire. For a while Brit lay there, feeling cozy and comfortable, listening to the children laugh and whisper to each other—to the women talk. Sigrid was the quiet one, very controlled, it seemed to Brit. Sif, on the other hand, chuckled and chattered and spoke of the neighbors, of what she had heard about this one or that one. Sif was the one who saw that Brit was awake. She looked over and smiled.

Brit smiled back. Then she rose, put on her boots, got a bra from her pack beneath the sleeping bench and excused herself to visit the lean-to. When she returned she washed her hands at the sink, enjoyed a big drink of water and turned to gesture at the two forlorn-looking piles of feathers lying on the table. "What have we here?"

"Eric brought them," said Asta, confirming what Brit had already guessed. "A pair of fine partridges. Aren't they beautiful?"

"They certainly are." She couldn't keep herself from asking, "He's been back again since morning, then? Eric, I mean."

Sif and Sigrid shared what could only have been called a sly, knowing look. Asta nodded. "He'll return for the evening meal."

Brit set her cup on the counter—firmly. Enough about Eric. "So how 'bout I make myself useful and pluck those birds for you?"

Asta tried to talk her out of it. It wasn't necessary, she said. She'd do it herself in a little while.

But Brit insisted. In the end, when she had sworn she could handle it, she was allowed to do the plucking. Eric had already gutted them in the field, which, her uncle Cam always said, was the best time to do it. The birds cooled faster that way; less chance the meat would sour.

"I'm guessing you have some sort of game shed," Brit said when the task was done.

Asta, still near the stove with her daughters-in-law, sent her an approving look. "We do. Out in the back."

Brit took them out and hung them in the wire cage behind the longhouse, where they'd be safe from scavengers until the meat had aged properly. When she returned, Sif was preparing to take Asta's laundry to the community washhouse.

Brit added her borrowed nightgown and a few other items to the big net bag. "I wonder—could I tag along?"

Sif, who had skin like fresh cream and wore her long red hair in two fat braids wrapped around her head, looked doubtful. "Are you certain you feel well enough?"

"Positive."

"She's a determined one," Asta remarked, never dropping a stitch. "Take her with you. Fresh air will bring the color back to her cheeks."

"I go, too," announced little Mist, rising from her seat on the floor and tucking her rag doll beneath her arm.

"All right," said her mother fondly. "You may come along."

"Don't overextend yourself," Asta told Brit. "If you tire, return immediately."

"You bet." Brit grabbed her coat from the peg and followed Sif and Mist out the door.

The washhouse was just beyond the bathhouse. Inside, there was running hot water and six deep concrete sinks, set up in pairs, one for washing, one for rinsing. Hooked between each pair of sinks were old-fashioned, hand-cranked clothes wringers. A washboard waited in each washing sink. Clotheslines ran everywhere, crisscrossing back and forth, about half of them hung with drying garments. One wall had a long table tucked against it—for folding the dry clothes, no doubt. And there were metal racks where sweaters, blocked back into shape, were drying.

Sif explained that each family had washhouse hours. They hung their clothes on the lines and came back for them after they'd had time to dry.

Brit wasn't much use at the wringer or the washboard. Her shoulder was still way too tender for that. But she helped feed the clothes into the roller while Sif cranked the handle. And then later, she shook out the wet things and handed them to Sif for hanging on the line.

And of course, while they worked, the two women talked. The usual getting-to-know-you chatter. Brit insisted she preferred to dispense with the Your Highnesses and asked how long Sif had been married and if she was born in the village.

"Gunnolf and I have been married eight years—and no, I come from a village to the east, near Solgang Fjord." Asta's wasn't the only village where the people known as Mystics made their home. There were several in the Vildelund.

Brit spoke of her sisters and their new husbands. And then she asked quietly, "Why is it neither Asta nor Eric will talk to me about my brother?"

Did the other woman's eyes shift away—just a fraction? After a moment Sif said carefully, "I think it's more that you were so insistent you'd seen him. They didn't know what to say about it, except to tell you that you couldn't have seen him, as he is dead."

He wasn't, of course. He lived. She knew it. She *had* seen him. But constantly insisting that she knew he was alive didn't seem to be getting her anywhere. A new approach was called for. "Did you ever meet my brother?" She shook out a wet shirt—from the size and cut, probably Eric's—and handed it to Sif.

Sif took so long to answer Brit began to think she wouldn't. But then she said, "For our wedding trip, Eric took Gunnolf and me over the Black Mountains to the south, to see Lysgard. We stayed for seven nights at Isenhalla. Gunnolf already knew your brother, since His Highness had visited this village often as a boy. But I had never had the honor." Sif hung the shirt on the line. Brit shook out a gray gathered skirt and glanced up to find Sif staring off toward the sinks, a musing smile on her full mouth. "It was a wondrous time for us. Newly wed. So happy. Looking forward to our life together here, in the village of Gunnolf's people. And being honored to tour our country's capital city as guests of the royal family."

Brit handed her the wet skirt. "You met Valbrand during that trip?"

"Yes. He was…so very handsome. And kind. Thoughtful for one so young—he was barely twenty at the time, I believe. On more than one occasion he paused to speak with Gunnolf and me. He would ask how we were enjoying our stay at Isenhalla. He even advised us on things to be sure to see in Lysgard." The blue eyes were misty. "Yes. I can tell you that." As opposed, Brit thought with some irony, to what you *can't* tell me? Sif sighed. "Prince Valbrand was a good man. What a king he would have made."

"Dawk Waiduh," said Mist. The child sat in a chair a few feet away, near the long table. She held her doll in her lap and she smiled proudly at Brit. "Pwince Vawbwand. Dawk Waiduh."

Sif gave a nervous laugh. "Children. The things they say…"

"What is a Dawk Waiduh?"

"Dawk Waiduh!" Mist insisted, as if Brit wasn't getting it right.

"She means Dark Raider, I think," Sif said, too casually, giving the gray skirt an extra shake, then turning to hang it on the line.

"Yes!" Mist was beaming again. "Dawk Waiduh."

Brit vaguely remembered hearing stories of the Dark Raider—way back when, at her mother's knee. Ingrid had made it a point that her California-raised daughters should know the myths, the basic history and at least some of the customs of the land where they were born. "A legend, right? A masked hero, all in black on a rare black Gullandrian horse."

"That's right," said Sif. "A legend. It is said that the Dark Raider is reborn to the people in troubled times to save them from corrupt men and tyrants without honor."

Dressed all in black, Brit was thinking. Both times Brit had seen her brother—those times that everyone kept insisting never happened—he'd been dressed in black. And that first time, well, hey, guess what? He'd been wearing a mask. She said lightly, "And the correlation between my brother and this legendary figure?"

Sif laughed again. "None that I know of—except in the mind of my two-year-old daughter."

Brit laughed, too. Then she looked at Sif sideways. "So tell me—seen the Dark Raider around the village lately?"

Sif blinked. Trapped, Brit thought. Hah!

And then, a gossip's gleam in her eye, Sif admitted, "I must confess, there have been…stories."

Brit leaned a little closer to Asta's daughter-in-law. "Tell me."

Sif waved a hand. "Oh, just rumors. Tall tales. An old man from three valleys over, attacked in the forest by thieves. He claimed the Dark Raider rescued him. And then there have been reports of a number of incidents involving renegades—you know about the renegades?" She must have seen by Brit's expression that she didn't. "You've been told that, in Gullandria, troubled youths are sent north, to our Mystic communities?''

"Yes." Just a month ago Brit's sister Liv had arranged to have a certain seventeen-year-old boy sent to the Mystics in hopes they might be able to help him change his ways.

"Sometimes," said Sif, "those difficult boys run away from us. They live wild, causing trouble whenever they come upon other people. We call them renegades."

Brit brought her hand to her injured shoulder, remembering the boy with the crossbow in Drakveden Fjord.

Sif was nodding. "Yes. The boy who shot you was a renegade." Brit had a few questions concerning that boy, but she didn't want Sif straying too far from the subject of the Dark Raider. Sif went on, "There have been stories of renegades stealing from local villagers, or groups of them coming in from the wild to wreak havoc on good folk. In a valley to the east of here, one renegade group is said to have staged a small reign of terror, threatening innocent people, killing livestock, breaking into longhouses when the owners were gone."

"And the Dark Raider stopped them?"

"Yes. The story goes that he caught them, one by one, that he took them where they could cause no more harm."

"And that would be where?"

"The Mystic village northernmost in all the Vildelund. We send the most incorrigible young ones there, to be shown—more forcefully—a better way."

"The boy who shot me—did Eric have him taken there?"

"I believe so. Yes."

"And the Dark Raider himself...if it's true he's returned, where would he be living now?"

Something happened in Sif's pretty face—a mental turning away. A retreat. Brit knew she was thinking she had said too much. "Eric would be the one to speak to of this." Asta's daughter-in-law bent to the pile of clothes, took out a nightgown, shook it and turned to hang it. "We must finish the laundry now."

Brit didn't press her further. She figured she'd gotten about as much as she was going to get from Sif, for the time being, anyway. And yes, it was all vague stuff. But it was vague stuff that matched up with what her own eyes had seen: a masked man in the fjord with Eric; her brother, in the longhouse, the same height and build as the man in the fjord, wearing the same black clothing.

And Eric warning him, "She sees you. She knows you. You shouldn't be here. Not without the mask...."

Now Sif spoke of an old legend come recently to life.

Was it totally crazy to imagine that her brother might have taken on the guise of the mythical Dark Raider? Not the way Brit saw it.

What better way to keep the fact that he still lived a secret from his enemies than to wear a mask?

Chapter Four

Another day passed. And another after that.

Brit's impatience was growing. She had come to the village for a reason. And since that one conversation with Sif Saturday afternoon in the washhouse, she hadn't moved a fraction of an inch toward her goal.

No one would talk to her. Not about Valbrand, anyway. The mention of his name brought long silences and significant looks. And then whoever she'd asked would answer that she already knew everything *they* knew on the subject.

She'd even gone so far as trying to get some small shred of information out of the children—and okay, that was kind of pitiful. But she was getting desperate.

They told her they'd seen Valbrand. That he came sometimes to visit—and that at night he turned into the Dark Raider. She almost got her hopes up, almost dared to imagine she might be getting somewhere.

But then the little darlings proceeded to tell her they'd also seen Thor in the sky, throwing his hammer, and Freyja riding through the clouds in her cat-drawn chariot.

So much for asking the kids.

Finally, on Tuesday, a week and a day after her plane went down, as she was sitting at the breakfast table with Asta and Eric, she decided she'd had about enough of getting nowhere. She looked across the table at the man who had carried her out of Drakveden Fjord.

Those haunting eyes were waiting, as usual. Over the past few days, she was constantly glancing up to find him looking at her, his gaze both measuring and intent.

Now he wore the strangest expression. Expectant and yet wary. As if he already knew what she would say.

"I would like to speak with you alone please—after breakfast if that's all right."

He nodded in that regal way of his. "As you wish."

And Asta beamed, as if the thought of the two of them speaking alone after breakfast just tickled her pink. "Well," the old woman said. "At last."

Now, what was for Asta to be so thrilled about? She had to know that they'd be talking about Valbrand.

Whatever was up with her, Asta couldn't get out and leave them alone fast enough. She had the table cleared and their breakfast bowls draining in the wooden rack on the counter in record time. "I'll be at Sigrid's," she announced breathlessly as she grabbed her heavy shawl from the row of pegs by the door.

Brit gave her a puzzled look and a wave as she went out.

The door clicked shut, and it was just Brit and Eric, facing each other across the plain wooden table.

"Well then." Those green-gray eyes looked at her probingly. "You have something to say to me?"

Something to say? Oh, you'd better believe it. She had a hundred questions, at least. Was it possible he was finally ready to fork over a few answers?

Jorund, the agent from the Gullandrian National Investigative Bureau she'd befriended, had warned her about this. "He's a Mystic through and through," the NIB special agent had cautioned. "Plays it close and tight. You'll have trouble getting anything out of him." But, hey. What did Jorund know? Hadn't he told her any number of times that she was chasing shadows, that her brother had met his end out there in the ocean, off the coast of Iceland somewhere? He'd been wrong on that count. Brit would prove him wrong about Eric, too.

She hoped.

Brit folded her hands on the table and leaned toward the silent man across from her. "You—and everyone else around here, as a matter of fact—keep claiming that my brother is dead, that I never saw him. Not here. Not in the fjord…" She let her voice trail off. Hey, who could say? Maybe he'd actually volunteer something. He didn't. "Well, okay, just for the sake of moving on, let's say that you're telling me the truth."

He nodded again. It wasn't an answer—but she hadn't really asked any questions. Yet.

"Okay, then, Eric. So let's go back aways."

"Back aways." He looked amused.

She quelled the urge to raise her voice in frustration and explained evenly, "That's right. If you won't admit my brother's alive, then will you tell me what you do know? Tell me what you found out, after he went missing. Tell me what you learned when you went searching for answers to what had happened to him."

"I learned nothing. Except that he is truly dead."

"Got that. But *how* did he die?"

"I'm sure your father must have told you."

"He did. But I want *you* to tell me. Please?"

He studied her for a long moment, then shifted on his bench and rested his forearms on the table. "The truth about Valbrand is exactly what His Majesty, your father, has told you. Valbrand went a-Viking—in the modern-day sense of the word, anyway. Every prince who plans to put himself forward as a candidate for the crown in the next kingmaking must accomplish such a journey. It is tradition. A holdover from the old days when kings themselves went a-Viking, when, as the old saying goes, 'Kings were made for honor, and not for long life.'

"Thus, Valbrand set out with a trusted crew in an authentic reconstruction of a Viking longship, from Lysgard harbor to the Shetland Islands, and on to the Faeroes. From there, he made for Iceland. Somewhere in the North Atlantic, he encountered a bad storm. During that storm, your brother was washed overboard, never to be seen again."

"And you know this for certain because?"

"I tracked down the survivors of the storm and spoke with them, in person. They told me what everyone already knows. I heard their stories and each one corroborated the one before. It all fit together and it all made sense. As I have told you time after time after time, I now have no doubt at all that Valbrand's death happened in a storm at sea." He leaned closer across the table. "There. Are you satisfied?"

"Never."

He made a low sound in his throat. "Freyja's eyes. When will you abandon this witless hope that you'll somehow find a dead man alive?"

Witless, huh? She was leaning forward, too. She leaned farther. They were nose to nose. The air between them seemed to crackle and snap. "I'll have you know that your own father—and mine—sent me here to try to find out what really happened to my brother."

"Is that what they told you?"

She scowled at him. "What do you mean, is that what they told me? Why else would I be here?" He was looking at her strangely again, frowning, his head slightly to the side. She reminded him, "And just in case you've somehow forgotten, my plane was *sabotaged*. And then there was that juvenile delinquent with the wicked-looking crossbow. Sif called him a renegade. Are you sure about that? Are you sure he wasn't someone sent by whoever messed with my plane, to finish me off in the event I managed to crawl out alive?"

Now he wore a patient look. "The boy was a renegade. One of a small number of ill-behaved young ruffians who roam the Vildelund committing murder and stirring up mayhem whenever they get the chance."

"So you're saying it was just the Gullandrian version of a random drive-by shooting? Oh, puh-lease. If you think I buy that, I've got a statue in New York harbor I can sell you.''

He seemed very sure. "The boy is a renegade. I spoke with him myself, before I sent him to the northernmost village where he'll receive the discipline and teaching he so obviously needs.''

"How did you manage that?''

"Manage what?''

"Well, you had me to drag out of there—and a wounded renegade to *send* to the north. I'm just trying to figure out how one man accomplished all that.''

"I was not alone. There were other men with me, men from the village. They took him north.''

"I didn't see any other men—well, except for my brother, all in black, wearing a mask.''

"Your brother is dead. He wasn't there.''

"He was. You and him and no one else.''

He shrugged. "The men were there, whether you saw them or not. And it's unfortunate that your plane crashed. But it doesn't mean the plane was sabotaged.''

"It was a fine plane in perfect working order. No way it would have gone to zero oil pressure out of nowhere like that.''

"Perhaps there was something wrong with your oil gauge—and as for why my father sent you here, we both know the reason. You have only to look as far as the medallion you wear around your neck to know the intentions of my father *and* yours.''

Brit stiffened. She felt for the chain at her neck and dragged the medallion out into the light. Her fingers closed around the warm, comforting shape of it.

"What are you talking about? Your father gave me this for luck, to keep me safe from all evil, he said."

Eric was wearing that odd expression again—that sort of bemused half frown, his head tipped to the side. "You really don't know, do you?"

"What?" she demanded. He went on looking at her. She said it again, louder, "*What?*"

And then, at last, he told her. "That medallion is mine. My father gave it to you so I might know you as my chosen bride."

Chapter Five

Should she have known? Probably.

"I see you have been...misled," he said softly. Brit only clutched the medallion and stared. Very patiently he went on, "We Mystics cling more closely to the old ways than do the people of the south. For us marriage is, first and foremost, an alliance between families. In the past millennium or so, it's been the custom for the father of the groom to present the future bride of his son with a special pendant—a marriage medallion that was wrought of silver in the first months after the son's birth. Each medallion is different, because each was made specifically for one treasured infant son."

He paused for a moment, his gaze holding hers. Then, as if he could see it, though she still had her hand wrapped around it and he continued looking right in her eyes, he said, "A circle in quadrants, a ribbon-like creature, twisting and twining over the whole—the world serpent, perhaps, that coils at the roots of the guardian tree, holding together all the nine worlds. Four animal heads—snakes, dragons, rams? Perhaps. Or perhaps these are creatures of fancy, of myth. And at the center, the symbol for Saint John's arms—like a cross, with four equal sides, each coiling and turning into the next. St. John is said to keep its bearer safe from all evil, did you know?"

She had, of course. Medwyn had told her—that much. But no more.

Eric said, "The medallion you wear used to hang on the wall above my blankets when I was an infant. As a child, I wore it against my flesh. When I turned eighteen, I gave it to my father—to be returned to me only around the neck of the woman I would wed. You."

It came to Brit, suddenly, why she hadn't figured it out before: she hadn't wanted to know. She'd been so proud and sure that her father and his grand counselor believed her—believed *in* her. That they'd seen her purpose and her determination to find her brother, or at the very least, to learn the truth of his death. She'd allowed herself to believe that they respected her quest—and yes, damn it, it *was* a quest.

But apparently, only to her. To them—to her father the king and Medwyn and this too-attractive man sitting opposite her, she was *only* a woman. And to them, as to far too many men, Gullandrian or otherwise, a woman was to be taken seriously in only one context.

In relationship to a man.

"Let me get this straight." She kept her voice low.

Moderate. Controlled. "Medwyn and my dad sent me here to *marry* you? I was almost killed in a plane crash, my guide *died,* I was just about finished off in a...a *hike-by* shooting, and you're trying to tell me it's all for the sake of *wedding bells?*"

"It is of great importance, whom you marry. The fate of our country may hang upon that choice."

"I'm not here to find a husband."

"Yet a husband is what you shall have."

"You can't force me to marry you."

"I will not have to force you."

She shoved back from the table, knocking the bench over behind her. The sound of it crashing to the floor was satisfying in the extreme. "Get this. I'll say it slowly. It's. Not. Going. To. Happen."

He frowned, just the slightest downward curl at each side of his fine mouth. "You are angry."

Major understatement. "You are right."

"You will come, over time, to accept—"

She raised a hand, palm out. "Uh-uh. Don't you even try to tell me what I'll accept."

He hadn't moved. He remained in his seat across the table, looking up, his expression patient enough to set her teeth on edge. "Perhaps now you wish to rest."

Rest after *this* conversation? "As if."

Shaking his head, he rose and carefully stepped free of the bench on his side of the table. "I fear there will be yelling and recriminations, if I stay."

"No kidding—and don't you dare leave yet."

He was already striding for the door.

She flew at him. "You are not walking out of here. Not now. Not until I say what I have to say." She grabbed his arm.

Big mistake. He stopped and looked right at her.

And there it was, that…energy. That…connection. Hot. And dangerously delicious.

Forget that, she told herself. She gave his arm a good yank and got her face right up to his, so she could stare squarely into those mesmerizing eyes. "He's alive, my brother. I know he is. I saw him. He was here, in this very room. He stood over my bed and he called me your *bride*. Now, how could I dream that, when I didn't know a thing about it until right now?"

Eric did not so much as blink. "Some things are known by the heart before they are known by the mind."

"Oh, don't give me that Mystic baloney. Valbrand's alive. Admit it."

"You delude yourself."

"The left side of his face is scarred. Terribly. What did that to him?"

"Turn your mind to what matters here."

"My brother. *He* is what matters. And I'm here to find him."

"Your brother is dead. Accept it. You are here because you are mine, as I am yours. The fates have decreed it."

"*Yours?* I don't even *know* you."

"You will. Over time."

"No."

He went on, not even pausing. "You are brave and strong. Of obvious intelligence, though sometimes too quick to act, when to watch and wait would be wiser. I have seen you with the children. You like them, you have a kind heart. To look at you pleases me. You are of a good age for breeding, though a bit younger might have been better.''

''Breeding? I'm a good age for *breeding?*''

''Overall, I am more than content with my father's choice—and I see in your eyes, in the quickening of your breath when you are near me, that I am not totally repellent to you.''

''This is insane.''

''No. This is as it was meant to be. It is our mutual fate that we be bound, each to the other, as man and wife.''

She let go of his arm and stepped back, mindful not to trip on the bench she'd overturned. ''Listen, it's not my fate to be *bound* to anyone. I need serious breathing room. For me, settling down goes under *later.* When I'm older. And slower. But by then, I won't be such a good *breeder,* will I? So from your point of view, what good would I be?''

He smiled at that, straight teeth flashing white. ''Your point is well taken. I have been too blunt. Months in the wilds will do that to a man. And it's always possible no children will come of our union. Yet there will be a union—in time. That much I know.'' His smile vanished. ''And it seems I have said too much too soon. You are not ready to hear the truth.''

She dragged in a long, dramatic breath and let it out slowly. ''Hear *that?* That's a deep sigh. It means, as I keep trying to tell you, that as far as this you-and-me thing goes—it's not. And it's never going to be.''

''It is.''

''It's not.''

He closed the distance she'd opened between them.

He did it slowly enough that he didn't spook her. Too bad. If he'd moved a little faster, she might have backed up. But she held her ground. And then he was right there, in front of her. His strong hand closed over hers.

Slowly he raised her hand to his lips.

She shocked herself. She let him do it. And when she felt his mouth against her skin, a hot and hungry shiver went shimmering through her.

"No!" She jerked away and cradled her hand as if he'd injured it. "Uh-uh. Not. No way…"

Eric made no effort to recapture her hand.

No progress was being made here.

Her fine eyes were wild, her wide mouth set in a scowl. He would very much have enjoyed kissing that mouth. But he'd had several days—to watch, to assess and to learn to admire; to accept the fact that this woman was meant for him. She had only just been informed of her fate, and that made her far from ready for kissing. For now he'd said what needed saying— and more. It was enough. He went to the door and put on his shearling coat, then took down the rifle racked beneath his shotgun.

She spoke then. "Wait."

He turned back to her slowly that time, holding the rifle with care, barrel to the floor.

She was guiding the silver chain over her head. "I'm not going to marry you, Eric." She held out the gleaming disk, the heavy chain trickling over her hand, the links falling through her fingers. "I want you to take this. Give it to the right woman when she comes along."

He felt again the urge to smile. This time he quelled it. "The right woman already has it."

Her face was flushed, blue eyes flashing. "Eric—" There was nothing to be gained by staying to hear more. He pulled open the door and went out.

Brit was left standing in the longhouse alone, the marriage medallion shining in her outstretched hand.

No problem, she thought, her fist closing tight over the silver disk. He won't take it. Doesn't matter. He's getting it back, anyway.

She marched over to his bed and dropped the medallion onto his furs, turning quickly away from it— from her own ridiculous reluctance to part with it. She righted the bench she'd kicked over and sat on it to put on her boots. Then she grabbed her jacket from its peg. She needed a long walk. A head-clearing dose of cold, fresh Vildelund air.

With her hand on the latch, she hesitated. No way strolling up and down the single village street, trying not to scowl at every friendly villager she happened to pass, was going to do the trick. She needed space and a total absence of other people. And if she was going to wander a little farther afield than the cluster of buildings that made up the tiny town, she'd be wise to do it armed. Renegades, apparently, *were* a problem around here. And from what she'd been told, there were bears. And wolves. And the legendary white Gullandrian mountain cats—and who knew what else?

Better armed than dead. She got her weapon from her pack, loaded it, put on her shoulder rig and holstered the SIG. Only then did she put on her coat and head for the door again.

Outside, it was in the high thirties. She felt in a

pocket and came up with that bag of peanut M&M candies that she'd opened before she climbed from her wrecked plane. She took one out—a red one—and put it in her mouth to savor. Delicious. She might want more. Maybe she'd eat them all on her walk, indulge in an orgy of chocolate and peanuts to soothe her frayed nerves, ease her troubled mind. She emptied them into the pocket and then wadded the bag and stuck it in the front pocket of her jeans to throw in the fire later.

Another pocket of her jacket yielded a wool beanie. A third, a pair of red wool gloves. She was pulling them on as she turned away from the street toward the back of the house, the M&M sweet in her mouth, her spirits already lifting.

At the rear of the house, about ten yards beyond the game cage, she reached a small barn. To either side of it rough plank fencing bordered a narrow paddock where a few horses grazed. One—a gelding with a dove-gray blaze between his big dark eyes—turned to watch as she climbed the fence and dropped to her feet inside. Then, with a snort that showed as mist on the icy air and a toss of his snow-white mane, he went back to cropping the short grass. None of the other horses seemed the least interested in her.

It was good, she decided, to be outside again, on her own, with the sun a rim of gold just making its climb over the crests of the hills to her right, the brown grass crackling with frost beneath her boots, the cold air sharp and bracing in her lungs and the inviting shelter of tall evergreens ahead.

She reached the back fence and hoisted herself over it with minimal awkwardness, though her left shoulder was still tender and any pressure on the muscles near the wound caused a definite twinge. When she dropped to the grass on the other side, she was perhaps thirty feet from the thick, close-growing forest of spruce that surrounded the village on all sides and grew up the flanks of the hills.

She stopped to press the compass button on her watch. The trees ahead were due north, Asta's house to the south. She should be safe to walk in the forest a little, as long as she was careful to keep her bearings and to watch out for predators—human or otherwise. She walked on into the shadows of the tall, proud trees, the thick blanket of short brown needles crunching underfoot.

The drop in temperature was immediate. Her breath came out as thick mist. She hunched down into the warmth of her jacket and picked up the pace a little—more exertion, more body heat.

A squirrel scolded her from a branch up ahead, tail twitching. She smiled as it jumped to the next tree, scampered inward to the rough red bark of the trunk and shot upward, vanishing from sight.

She felt better already. It was good, to be alone for a while, outside in the clean air, with only the sentinel trees and the chattering squirrels for company.

Her M&M was down to the peanut. Brit bit it good and hard and chewed it to a pulp. She swallowed. The situation stunk. There was Eric, who was too sexy and too tempting—and had some crazy idea that the two of them were meant for each other. And there were Asta and her daughters-in-law, sending Brit hopeful, dreamy-eyed looks every time Eric's name was mentioned. Worst of all, there was her father, who had tricked her into thinking he believed in her quest—well, no. Worst of all was the quest itself, her search for her lost brother, which was going nowhere fast.

"Take 'em off, sweetling."

Brit froze on the shadowed path. The voice, from up ahead, was male, unfamiliar—and full of youth and meanness.

"I am not your sweetling, lout." A woman's voice. Angry. Proud.

Someone laughed, low and harsh. And then came another voice, male and young, like the first, but more nasal. "We have you. Surrender."

"Never."

A silence. And then the unpleasant sound of a fist hitting flesh. A grunt. Scuffling.

"Hold her, Trigg…"

"Loki mock her, she's slippery as an angry otter…"

The blows and grunts continued. Brit didn't like to shoot with gloves on, but there was no time to remove them. She drew her SIG, levered back the safety. Carefully, gun at the ready, she crept forward toward the sound. At the next curve in the path, she came upon them. Two boys—renegades, no doubt.

And one young woman, dressed much like them, in rawhide leather, high lace-up moccasin-like boots on her feet. The woman struggled against the grip of the larger boy as the other tore at her clothes.

Rape in progress? Apparently.

Her pulse pounding in her throat, Brit acted. What else was there to do? She stepped out into the open, gun straight out, aiming steady with both hands. "Stop. Now."

The boys froze and turned. "Balls of Balder, who are *you?*" demanded the one with the nasal voice.

Brit gestured, a twitch of the gun barrel. "Hands up. Now."

The boys, looking sullen and snarly, did as instructed.

"On the ground," Brit said. "Facedown." The boys dropped to a sprawl. "Spread your arms wider. And your legs." They complied.

The woman, whose blond hair had come loose from a thick braid, and half-covered her face, spared not more than a glance at Brit. She seemed totally unmoved by what had almost happened to her. "I'll bind them."

Brit didn't argue. "Great idea."

The woman, who was about Brit's size, was already striding to a leather pack that waited on the ground a few feet away. She dropped to her haunches and took out several lengths of leather twine. Brit held her gun on the pair as the woman swiftly and expertly tied their hands and ankles.

When she finished, she stood tall and spat on the ground between the two would-be rapists. "There. That'll hold 'em." She raked her wild hair off her face and looked directly at Brit for the first time.

Brit gasped. "My God."

The woman had an ugly cut on her full lower lip, a deep scratch on her cheek and an angry bruise rising at her jawline. But it wasn't her injuries that had Brit staring, openmouthed. It was the woman herself.

Injuries aside, she was the image of Brit's mother. She was Ingrid Freyasdahl Thorson, just as she looked in the old pictures in the family albums at home. Brit's mother. Twenty-plus years ago.

How could that be?

"Princess Brit?" The woman smiled. It was Brit's mother smiling, Brit's mother in her midtwenties, with a cut lip and a naughty gleam in her sea-blue eyes. "Don't answer," she said. "There's no need. I know you by the look of you. And isn't this a story to be told around the tent fire on a cold winter's night? The gods must be pleased with us. They have sent you out to meet us."

Us?

Right then, from directly behind Brit, another woman said, "Drop your weapon, Your Highness. Or I'll be forced to send my arrow flying straight to your heart."

Chapter Six

One hand in the air, Brit knelt and carefully set the SIG on the ground. Still grinning, the woman who looked like her mother darted forward and snatched it up.

She pointed it at Brit. "Got her, Grid."

The other woman—Grid?—came around in front of her, an arrow in her bow, but pointed at the ground. She was much older than the first woman, with graying brown hair, broad shoulders and thick legs. "By the wolves of Odin, Rinda," she said. "I dare not leave you on your own for the span of a minute."

Rinda shrugged. "No real harm done. And look who has come to my aid."

"Of that," said Grid, "I cannot complain."

Brit cleared her throat. "Look. I'm on *your* side. There's no need for you to take my—"

"Silence," barked Grid.

"But I only—"

Three words. That was as far as she got. By then Grid had drawn her free hand across her barrel chest. *Smack*. The back of Grid's hand caught Brit hard on her right cheek. Brit went spinning. She landed on her face in the dirt.

"Get up," growled Grid. "And don't speak again unless you are first spoken to."

The whole right side of Brit's face felt numb. Lovely. Brit brought her hands up to push herself to her knees. Her right hand brushed against a few hard little balls—M&Ms, fallen from her pocket as she dropped. She managed to drag them along with the back of her glove and to grab them in her fist before she scrambled upright. Neither of the women seemed to notice. Good. She really needed them. Nothing like a peanut M&M when a girl was under stress....

Eric checked his traps in the woods east of the village, finding one angry white fox. He released it, chiding himself for a too-soft heart.

Then, hoping the rage of his reluctant bride would have cooled somewhat by then, he returned to his aunt's longhouse. The women were there, clustered near the fire, busy with their sewing, the children playing quietly around them. There was one woman missing.

The most important one.

The others looked up from their stitching and saw him. A small silence followed, one brimming with expectation.

Asta broke the silence. "Why, where's Brit?"

"Bwit," said little Mist, who was sitting on the floor near Eric's sleeping bench. "Gone, gone, gone."

Eric frowned. "She was here when I left."

The women shared quick glances. Sif said, "And we assumed she was with you."

He looked at the pegs by the door. Her big blue jacket wasn't there. Her boots should have been waiting on the floor beneath the missing jacket. They weren't there, either.

The women were shaking their heads.

Mist had gotten to her plump little feet beside his sleeping bench. She reached for something among the furs and then held up a silver chain. His marriage medallion turned at the end of it. "Ohh, pwetty, pwetty."

Eric approached the child and knelt before her. "Mist. That is mine."

Mist frowned, but then, with a long sigh, she offered the chain. "Ewic take."

He plucked the dangling medallion from the air, winking at the winsome child as he rose. He slipped the chain over his neck and tucked the silver disk beneath his leather shirt. When Brit wanted it back, it would be waiting, warm from his body, charged with all the energy his strong heart could give it.

Right now, though, he had to find where the irksome woman had gotten herself off to.

Asta and his cousins' wives were watching him.

"Asta," he said. "Stay with the children. Sif. Sigrid. Come and help me find my runaway bride."

Eric and his cousins' wives searched the village, knocking on every door, looking through the bathhouse and the washhouse, the various small barns and other outbuildings. When they'd checked everywhere to no avail, he and the women returned to his aunt's house, where they found the older children playing outside near the front step.

Asta signaled him inside—alone. "Word has come."

Mist was sitting under the long deal table, cradling her yarn-haired doll. "Dawk Waiduh," she said, with a happy little laugh.

Asta said, "In the woods just north of the back pasture you'll find a pair of renegades. They are bound hand and foot—and they have quite a tale to tell."

The two women had horses. They rode bareback. Brit, her hands tied before her, rode double with the one named Rinda. Grid took the lead.

There had been little explanation. They were taking her to their camp, they said. The news of Brit's arrival over a week ago had spread through the Vildelund. The two women had been sent to the village in search of her.

It didn't take a Mensa candidate to figure out what they were. Anyone who knew anything of Gullandria had heard the tales of the *kvina soldars*—the nomadic warrior women who lived in the Vildelund, who fought with great skill and lived free, never binding their lives to any man. As a child at her mother's knee, Brit had loved to hear the tales of the *kvina soldars*. In her soft bed in her mother's house in Sacramento, she used to dream of someday coming to her father's land, of traveling to the wild north country, of meeting a *kvina soldar* face-to-face.

Well. Be careful what you dream of, as they say.

Brit had the front position on the sturdy mare, her "cousin's" slim body pressed close at her back. They'd been on the trail, moving mostly northeast and climbing, for over an hour.

Brit was following Grid's orders and staying quiet. She concentrated on the easy rhythm of the horse beneath her. Riding came natural as breathing to her, always had. Her legs did the work, so even with her hands tied, she had little trouble keeping her seat. For balance, she wrapped her fingers in the mare's braided mane. She listened to the sound of the wind in the tall trees, felt the warmth of the woman who might be a lost cousin at her back—and she tried not to worry.

Strangely, it wasn't so hard not to worry about herself. She'd looked into the eyes of both Rinda and Grid and seen no cruelty there. They were tough women, women who lived by their wits, their strength and their fighting skills. Her instinctive assessment of their basic decency had been bolstered by the way they ended up dealing with the two renegade boys.

To the *kvina soldars,* from what Brit had learned as she sought to understand the different peoples of her father's land, rape was a crime punishable by death. And not only that. After killing a rapist, the warrior women frequently mutilated the man's body, cutting off both his head and his offending male parts.

By their lights, Grid and Rinda had every right to kill the renegade pair. But they hadn't. They'd decided to leave them to the mercy of chance. Whoever—or whatever—found them, would get to deal with them. To Brit this seemed more than reasonable, given the circumstances.

It was less reasonable of the women to carry Brit

off. After all, she'd done nothing but come to the aid of one of them. They might have been a little grateful and let her head back to Asta's place in peace.

But no. Their "leader" wished to speak with her. And their job was to make that happen. What Brit wanted counted for nothing with them.

From overhead came the cry of a hunting bird. Brit glanced up to see a hawk soaring in the clear blue, and she thought of that other hawk in Drakveden Fjord the day this big adventure had begun.

She thought of Eric's face that first time she'd seen him in person, of the worry in his eyes as he'd looked down at her—injured, fading fast, on the rocky, cold ground. Now she was the one worrying. For him. Because Eric was going to blame himself when he found out she was missing.

Their disagreement back at the longhouse seemed of no importance now. So what if he thought they were getting married? It didn't matter, let him think it. What mattered was that Eric Greyfell was the kind of man who took his responsibilities seriously. He would consider it his duty to keep her safe and he would torture himself for failing in his duty.

He was an exasperating man. But still, she didn't want him torturing himself.

He would come after her, of course—at least, he would if he could figure out where to look. She was doing what she could to help him with that, though she doubted her little attempt to lead him along would work. But it seemed only right to at least give it a try.

She was thinking of it as the "Hansel and Gretel" technique. Instead of a trail of bread crumbs or pebbles to show the way, she was dropping peanut M&Ms. So far she'd dropped three. One in the clearing just as they were leaving. One about twenty minutes later. And one several minutes after that.

Okay, it was kind of pitiful if she gave it too much thought. What were three little M&Ms in an hour's worth of traveling? Not a lot. But hey, she was doing the best she could with what she had.

And as of now, her hands were empty.

For the first time since Grid backhanded her for talking, she dared to speak. "Ahem. Sorry, but I really have to have a moment in the bushes."

Neither Grid nor Rinda responded. The horses labored upward on the trail. Perhaps five minutes passed. Brit was debating how soon she dared to ask again, when Grid pulled to a stop. "Right there." Grid pointed at a clump of bushes beside the trail. "Relieve yourself. Make no sudden movements. We will be watching."

Terrific. Should she ask to have her hands untied? Uh-uh. If they did free her hands for the moment, they would only tie them again before she got back on the horse. And then they would be too likely to spot her trick.

Brit went into the bushes. It was quite the fun adventure, getting her pants down with her hands tied and the wool gloves making her fingers all fat and awkward. Lots of wiggling and squirming involved.

Which actually worked out fine. All the jerking around provided cover for that split second after she had her pants back up and zipped, when she shoved both hands in her jacket pocket and got what she needed.

Two minutes later she was back on the horse. She

waited several minutes more before she let the next M&M roll from her fisted hand.

Twenty minutes after her break in the bushes, they reached the crest of the hill they'd been climbing. Below them the land fell away sharply into a deep tree-shrouded ravine. They started down, moving west, then switching back, going east, following the zigs and zags of the trail as it took them to the bottom.

At the bottom, they crossed a swift-running stream and started climbing again. At the top of that hill, they went down in a series of switchbacks, the same as before.

And so on, for hours.

Finally, in late afternoon, they descended another hill and began moving east along the narrow strip of relatively flat land at the bottom. They were deep in the trees. Brit hunched into her jacket and shivered and let go of another M&M. After that she had only one left.

It was perhaps ten minutes later—by then she was tired enough she hardly glanced at her watch anymore—that another woman, dressed much like Rinda and Grid but with skin the color of richest mahogany, materialized from the bushes at the side of the trail. The woman stood, hands on hips, dark eyes flashing, squarely in their path.

"Greetings, sisters."

Grid reined in and saluted, the tips of her fingers to the center of her forehead. "Freyja guide your sword arm, Fulla guard your hearth."

"You have her," said the woman on the trail.

"We do."

"Come, then. Ragnild awaits."

The warrior on the trail turned and vanished into the trees. Grid—and Rinda and Brit—followed. Brit let go of the final piece of candy, right there, a few yards after they turned into the trees.

They all three had to duck low to the horses to keep from being unseated by the thick, low-hanging branches. They rode for five minutes or so, Grid and Brit with cheeks to the necks of their mounts, Rinda with her head pressed against Brit's side.

At last, the trees opened up into a clearing: the camp of the *kvina soldars*.

Brit saw teepee-style tents arranged in a circle, smoke spiraling up through the tops of them. In addition to whatever fires burned within, there were open fires, rimmed by rocks, before the tents. Beyond the tent circle, hobbled horses nibbled the short grass. Warrior women of various ages moved in and out of the tents. Some of the women were black, some were of Asian descent, some Middle Eastern. There were dogs. And there were children, two of whom—at first glance, anyway—appeared to be little boys. In the center of the circle, someone had pounded in a tree trunk about a foot in diameter and around seven feet tall.

Grid dismounted.

"Get down," said Rinda from behind her.

Stiffly—after all that time riding bareback with bound hands—Brit slid to the ground. Rinda dismounted last. The dark-skinned woman who had found them on the trail led the horses off.

"This way," said Grid.

Brit fell in step behind her. Rinda took up the rear. Grid led them across the central area between the tents, to one slightly larger tent on the eastern side of the circle. As they passed, the children stopped their play to stare. The other women either ignored the new-comers or paused to salute, fingers to forehead, as Grid had done on the trail.

At the tent, they ducked inside.

A woman waited beyond the central fire, on the far side of the tent. She wore a white leather robe over her clothing. The robe was decorated with red runic-looking symbols. She sat cross-legged on a pallet of furs. Her hair was auburn, loose and full around her handsome face. Brit would have guessed her to be about forty.

"Unbind her," the woman in the robe commanded.

Grid turned to Brit, a knife in her hand. One clean swipe and the leather thongs fell away. Brit slid off her gloves, stuck them in a pocket and rubbed her tender, leather-abraded wrists.

The woman in the robe saluted Grid and Rinda. "Thank you. You may leave her here with me."

"But—" Rinda began.

The woman on the pallet cut her off with a slow shake of her head. "Discipline, my daughter. The first cornerstone of a life of power."

Rinda said nothing more. She followed Grid out.

"Do you thirst?" asked the auburn-haired woman. "Do you have need to relieve yourself?"

Brit was not at her best by then. Her thighs ached and her shoulder throbbed and she hadn't a clue where she was or what was going to happen next. Also, if she'd thought the Mystic villagers lived primitively, well, hel-lo. The *kvina soldars* had them beat by a mile. "Do I get to talk now?"

The handsome woman frowned. "You are angry?"

"Uh, yeah. You could say that. There I was, walking in the woods, minding my own business. And I come upon what is about to be a rape. I step in, stop the rape—and get kidnapped for my trouble." She touched her cheek. "Plus, Grid backhanded me for asking questions about what, exactly, was happening. And no, I don't have to relieve myself and we stopped to drink at a spring not far back down the trail."

The woman gestured at her pallet, which was big enough for more than one. "Please. Will you sit? I apologize for the…zealousness of my women. I requested that they bring you to me. They only did what I asked of them."

"So you're saying you're the one to blame?"

The woman smiled, the fine lines around her eyes etching deeper. "Yes. I am Ragnild, leader of this camp. And I am to blame for everything. Now. Will you sit?"

Brit blew out a breath. "I suppose." She circled the low fire and dropped to the furs with a tiny groan. She really wasn't used to riding without a saddle. Everything was going to be way sore by tomorrow. But back to business. "Okay, Ragnild. What is going on?"

The woman put up a hand. "Please. Be still now. Look me squarely in the eye."

Brit stifled a second groan—one that had nothing to do with her physical discomfort. She wanted answers, damn it. And she deserved them.

But something in the leader calmed her. Made her willing to just sit there—for a moment, anyway—and stare straight into Ragnild's hazel eyes.

"Yes," said Ragnild, after a long, strangely peaceful span of time. "It is as my dreams have foretold. You will be a great queen, the first in our nation's history to rule *with* her king."

Chapter Seven

Brit opened her mouth to argue—but decided against it. What Ragnild predicted would happen or it wouldn't. And the future wasn't the issue right now.

Now she had questions. Lots of them. "Rinda called me her cousin…"

"Because you are. As I am her mother."

"But how are we related?"

"Your mother had a brother named Brian. Have you been told of him?"

Brit made a face. "More than I wanted to know, to be honest." Her mother had finally told Liv, only weeks ago, why she had left their father, why she had split their family in two—baby triplet daughters to Ingrid, sons to Osrik. Brian Freyasdahl, a real piece of work, as it turned out, had been at the center of the problem. She frowned. "You're saying that my rotten uncle Brian was Rinda's father?"

Ragnild sighed.

Brit understood. "You're the one, aren't you? The one who killed him, the one who cut off his head and his—"

Ragnild waved a hand. "It was long ago."

"But then…he must have raped you, right?"

"He did. And for that I did what any *kvina soldar* will do to a man who dares to take what it is a woman's sacred choice to give. A few months later I realized that I would have his child."

She thought of Rinda, with her bold attitude and her naughty smile. "That makes your daughter illegitimate."

Ragnild nodded. *"Fitz,"* she said softly, with distaste. In Gullandria, a bastard child was called a *fitz* and was considered the lowest of the low. "Among us, among the warrior women, there is no judgment on the child for being born outside of a marriage. No *kvina soldar* can marry and remain with us, anyway. Sometimes, for whatever reason—the dishonor of rape, the lusts of the flesh, the true call of love—we find ourselves with child. When that happens, should we choose to have the child, we love that child and bring her or him up strong and capable and proud, as much as we can." She smoothed the soft white leather of her robe. "With girl children, it usually works well, since they most often choose to stay with us. The life of the boys is more difficult. They are sent away at the age of eight and they suffer at the cruelty of the outside world."

Brit was thinking of her brother-in-law, the king's warrior, Hauk Wyborn. Her father had recently legitimized Hauk, but before that Hauk's last name had been *Fitz*Wyborn. "My brother-in-law's mother was a *kvina soldar*."

Ragnild smiled softly. "Valda Booth. I knew her. She was a great warrior."

And really, there were more important things to be talking about than the plight of the *fitz* in Gullandrian society and what a dirty rat her creepy long-dead uncle had been. "What do you know of my brother, Valbrand?"

If the abrupt change of subject bothered Ragnild, she didn't show it. "They say he died at sea."

"Do you believe that?"

"Shouldn't I believe it?"

"I don't. I think someone tried to kill him. And I know in my heart that that someone failed."

"The heart is often wiser than the mind."

"So you're saying you think I'm right?"

"I am saying that you must do…what you must do."

"You know, you're like a lot of people in Gullandria. Big dreams of what the future will be, not very helpful in the here and now."

Ragnild chuckled. "I fear you speak the truth."

Brit sent her cousin's mother a sideways look. "What about the Dark Raider? Heard any stories about him showing up in the Vildelund lately?"

Ragnild nodded. "Rumor has it he rides among us again—that he rescued an old man from thieves, that he dealt with a group of renegades who were terrorizing one of the nearby Mystic communities."

Okay, great. Ragnild had heard the same stories as Sif. A confirmation. But nothing new. "Another question."

"Ask."

"When am I allowed to go back to the village where I came from?"

"Will tomorrow be acceptable? You'll stay with us tonight, share a meal, get to know your cousin a little. Rinda and Grid will take you back in the morning."

"So…this is it, then? You had me abducted so you could look in my eyes and reassure yourself that your dreams will come true?"

Ragnild laughed full out. It was a strong, rich sound. "I fear you have it exactly right—to look in the eyes of our future queen, to forge, you might say, the beginnings of a bond between us, for the sake of the future of my women. And to meet my daughter's blood cousin. I find I am well satisfied, on all counts."

Brit grumbled, "Rinda took my SIG 220, you know. I'm really fond of that gun."

"I'll have it returned to you immediately."

"Good. But getting my pistol back isn't the only problem. There are people who have to be seriously freaked by now, worrying about me."

"You'll return to them tomorrow, none the worse for wear."

Brit got a tour of the village and a lesson in the practice of the dragon dials.

The dragon dials was an exercise system developed in the seventeenth century by the *kvina soldars*. It was a specific sequence of slow, controlled movements that the warrior women believed promoted strength, calmness, discipline and mental clarity.

After the exercise session, Brit shared a meal in Ragnild's tent with the camp leader, Rinda, Grid and several other women. They had reindeer stew. Brit found it tasty, if a little tough. After the meal, Rinda invited Brit to the hot springs not far from camp.

Brit went gratefully, looking forward to soothing the aches and pains from a long day on the trail. Rinda brought a fresh dressing along for Brit's shoulder wound and changed it for her once they'd had a long soak.

Really, Brit was feeling pretty good about everything as she and Rinda strolled back to camp. Tomorrow she'd return to Asta's place.

And the day after tomorrow, she was heading out again. For Drakveden Fjord. It was time to have a look at what was left of the Skyhawk, to see if she could find a clue as to who had sabotaged her plane.

They heard the commotion as they came out of the trees and into the clearing where the circle of tents stood. Something was going on in the center of the circle.

Rinda grinned. "Looks to me like they've caught a man."

Brit walked faster—and stopped dead when she saw.

They certainly had caught a man. And that man was Eric. He was tied to the big stake in the center of the circle. The children of the camp darted around him, taunting him, and now and then striking him with stones and sticks.

Brit took off at a run. "Hey, stop that!" She hit the center of the circle yelling, making shooing motions with her hands. "Cut that out, you little brats. Go on, go on. Get away from him!"

The children backed off, though a couple made grotesque faces and stuck out their tongues.

Brit turned to Eric. "Are you all right?"

"Most assuredly," he replied. His expression was subdued. She couldn't read his eyes. "Especially now that my champion is here."

She grunted. "Oh, yeah, right."

About then, Ragnild emerged from her tent. "There you are. We've been awaiting you. This man has said your name in hopes that you might claim him."

"This man is...my friend. He's only here to rescue me. Untie him. Now."

Ragnild was shaking her head. "I regret that I can't do that—at least, not yet."

"Why the hell not?"

"This man strode boldly into the center of our camp. No man is allowed such a liberty. And he can't even plead ignorance. I know him. He is the son of the grand counselor, born of Mystic stock. He knows our ways."

Brit turned to Eric. A trickle of blood slid down his neck where some cruel child had struck him. "What is she talking about?"

Instead of an answer, she got one lifted sable eyebrow.

Argh. What was up with him? He could help her out a little here. She faced her aunt again. "I'm afraid I'm confused. *Why* is he tied up? What did he do?"

Ragnild was frowning. "I have explained that. He belongs to no woman here, yet he dared to walk boldly among us. Such behavior cannot be allowed."

Rinda stepped forward. She was grinning that naughty grin of hers. "You have to claim him." She tipped her head to the side and looked Eric up and down. "Hmm." She licked her split lip. "Perhaps I shall claim him—that is, cousin, should you reject him first."

"What is this? *Claim* him? How do I do that?"

"You say, 'I will claim this man.'"

"Okay. And then?"

"Then we untie him. You take him to your tent— Grid and I shall be pleased to have you borrow ours."

"Okay. I take him to my tent…"

"And then—" Rinda's grin widened "—you have your way with him."

"My *way?*"

Rinda laughed. "You do take my meaning. I see it in your eyes."

Brit sighed. "And after I have my way with him?"

"Then you may keep him for as many as seven nights, though I suppose, in your case, it would only be the one night, as tomorrow you are leaving us. If you are pleased with his performance, it is the custom that you let him go." Rinda's grin got wider. "If he doesn't please you, you can offer him to another of us. Or simply kill him for being useless as a lover."

Bizarre. "And what if I *don't* claim him?"

"Well then, if no one else wants him, we'll kill him right now."

"You're not serious."

No one said anything. Ragnild looked determined. Rinda continued to look way too amused. The blood-thirsty children watched with wide, eager eyes. And Eric simply waited, his angular face a patient mask. As if it made no difference to him whether she took him or the warrior women stabbed him in the heart.

Finally Ragnild asked somberly, "Cousin to my only daughter, will you claim this man?"

The choices were severely limited. "Okay, all right. I claim this man."

Chapter Eight

"What are you, nuts?" Brit demanded. "I really think they might have killed you." They were alone in the tent Grid and Rinda had given them for their supposed night of sexual delights.

Eric stood over the low central fire, warming his hands. Firelight glinted off his clubbed-back hair, bringing out bronze gleams in the ash-brown strands. "No harm is done, for you have saved me."

Was he *smiling?* Brit swore, a very bad swear word. "You have blood on your neck."

"And you have a new bruise on your cheek."

Lightly she touched the swollen spot where Grid's knuckles had struck. "I spoke when not spoken to."

"A good thing you don't receive a blow every time you do that."

"Chuckle, chuckle."

He took a handkerchief from the pocket of his shearling coat and wiped until only a faint smear remained. "Better?" He stuck the cloth back in his pocket.

"Not particularly. How can you stand there and grin? That was stupid, what you did. Those women out there take their beliefs seriously."

"I had complete faith in you."

"What if I wasn't here, what if I hadn't come back to the camp, for some reason? What if I had refused to claim you?"

"But you *were* here. You *did* come back...and you *have* claimed me." That haunting deep-set gaze was on her.

She felt her skin grow warmer, felt the hungry shiver sliding through her. "Stop that."

"Stop what?"

"You know what. That...look. You give me that look and I get all..." She let the sentence die unfinished, since she was getting herself deeper in trouble with every word.

He showed no mercy. "You get 'all' what?"

"Just...don't, okay?"

"Don't...?"

She flung out both hands. "Don't give me the bedroom eyes. Don't get...ideas."

"Bedroom eyes? You Americans. Such amusing figures of speech." He took something from another pocket, then shrugged out of the coat and tossed it on the pallet that lay against the side of the tent, to his left. His leather shirt was the same one he'd been wearing that morning. It had lacings at the neck. She could see a slice of firm, smooth chest.

And a few links of silver chain, shining. "I see you found your medallion."

"Would you like it back now?"

"Uh. No, I would not."

He circled the fire and came toward her. She debated: shrink back or stand proud?

As usual, before she made a choice, there he was. Right in front of her, mesmerizing eyes and broad shoulders filling the world. "Give me your hand."

"I said I don't want the medallion."

"I have something else of yours."

She should probably take issue with the word *else*. Then again, better not to belabor a point made far too many times already. She settled for a sneering curl to her lip and a surly, "What?"

He simply waited.

"Oh, all right." Grudgingly she held out her hand.

He cradled her palm, his hand warm and firm around the back of hers.

The problem was, she did like it. When he touched her. She gloried in the shivery feelings he aroused, though she kept trying to tell herself she shouldn't, that her obvious response to him only egged him on when it was absolutely paramount that she keep him at a distance.

Carefully, so as not to spill them, he laid a pile of peanut M&Ms in her cupped hand.

She looked down at them and back up at him. He was smiling again. And so was she—now. It was just too rich. "Pretty good, huh?"

"You are a woman of greatest resourcefulness."

"That I am."

"Not that I wouldn't have found you without the

bright-colored trail you left for me. I would find you anywhere."

"Oh, I'll bet."

The fire behind him crackled cheerily. Thin gray curls of smoke drifted up through the tent hole above. Outside, faintly, she could hear the sounds of the women of the camp as they prepared to settle in for the night. A woman called for a child and a thin voice answered, "Coming, Mama!" Brit stared at Eric and he stared back at her and they smiled at each other like a couple of fools.

"I was curious," he said. "I ate one."

"Did you like it?"

"It was excellent. That smooth outer shell, the silky, melting ball of chocolate, the crunch of the nut within…"

He had it exactly. She confessed, though it was the last thing she ought to be telling him, "I like to suck them. Slowly."

He whispered, his voice rubbing, velvet soft, along her every nerve, "Show me."

She made herself frown. "Oh, puh-lease. They've been on the ground."

"So fastidious…"

"That's me." She was thinking of that big plate of night crawlers in blood balls she'd lapped up that time on *Fear Factor*. Fastidious. Oh, yeah. Fershure. At least when she could afford to be.

She noticed that he was bending his head.

And yes, it was true. She was lifting hers.

Their lips met.

Well, what do you know?

She was doing it. Kissing Eric, though she knew she shouldn't.

Okay, all right. It was a problem she had. Just ask her mother. There was always what she *should* be doing: college, finishing one of her novels, stuff like that. And the various dangerous activities that tempted her: to learn to fly, to earn a black belt, to explore what was left of the world's wildernesses, the kinds of places where if you didn't know what you were doing, you could end up dead.

Oscar Wilde had said it best: "I can resist everything except temptation…"

You go, Oscar!

His mouth to hers…so lightly. Just brushing. And what a mouth it was. Exactly as she'd imagined it, velvety soft as his voice could be.

He spoke between those brushing kisses. "My dreams. At last. Coming true."

She pulled back. "Don't get your hopes up. It was only a—"

He silenced her by taking her mouth again. She let him do it.

Only a kiss, she promised herself. It's only a bone-melting, sweet, tender kiss….

Oh, and it was…all that.

Really, she had to be honest—at least, with herself. *He* was…all that.

His lips settled in, covering the whole of her mouth. She heard an eager, needful sound—a sound that came from her own throat. And her mouth was opening—just a little, she promised herself. Only enough to let in the wonderful moist heat of his breath.

But then, what do you know? His tongue came in, too. And she didn't close her lips against it.

In fact, she slid her own tongue beneath his.

Oh, my, yes.

Their tongues sparred and slid, up and over each other. His retreated.

Hers followed. Into the wet cave beyond those beautiful, tempting, velvet-soft lips.

Chaka-boom, she was going.

Going, going...

Gone.

With a hungry cry, she grabbed for him, wincing a little as her hurt shoulder complained. She slid her eager hands up over his hard chest, his strong shoulders, until she had him around the neck, until her body was pressed to his, her breasts to his chest, her hips just below his. Against her belly she could feel his desire. Heaven, that hard ridge. At the center of herself, she was warming, softening, hollowing out. Melting like the chocolate beneath the outer shell of an M&M, the sweetness spreading...

She opened her hand. The candies rolled down his back and hit the dirt floor with soft plopping sounds.

He chuckled at that.

She pulled back enough to grant him a mock scowl. "You know we shouldn't be doing this."

He laid a finger against her mouth. "No. You have it wrong. We *must* do this. I must please you. Or you'll have to kill me."

She stuck out her tongue and licked that finger of his—it tasted salty and a little bit dusty. Altogether lovely.

Fastidious? Brit Thorson? Not right this minute...

She felt his low groan as it rose from his chest. Delicious. Perfect.

No, she would not marry him, no matter what the fates predicted. But this…

How could she turn away from this?

He brought up his other hand and cradled her face in his warm, cherishing palms. His eyes looked into hers. She was falling. Down and down…

"You have claimed me. You shall have me."

Oh, well. All right.

But then again…

"I have an idea." Her voice came out husky, hungry, low.

"Share it."

"How 'bout we don't? And just say we did."

He only shook his head at that, his eyes so deep, his mouth swollen with kissing.

Crazy, she told herself. Way, way insane.

A leather strip held back his hair—another temptation, more of the only thing she couldn't resist. She took that strip and pulled. It slid away. His hair fell loose around his shoulders. She let the bit of leather drop, down there to the dirt, with the scattered M&Ms. She combed her fingers through the strands—so silky, alive with the warmth of him.

"You don't need this coat," he said.

She didn't argue. She let him push it from her shoulders and toss it to the pallet where his own coat lay.

He gathered her close again, enfolding her in those lean, strong arms. And he kissed her, his tongue pushing in, finding hers waiting. To welcome him.

To play…

He had her sweater by the sides. He raised it, fingers

trailing over the bumpy fabric of her thermal shirt, thrilling her with the simple pressure of his touch. The kiss was interrupted as he pulled the sweater over her head. She lifted her arms straight up too fast.

A small cry of pain got away from her.

He tossed the sweater away, his brows drawing together. "Your wound...?"

"No. Nothing. It's..."

But he was bending close again, pressing his lips to her shirt, right over the bandage that covered the place where the arrow had struck. He blew out a breath. She felt it through the layers of cloth and the bandage. It was lovely. Warm and moist. So tender. So soothing. So right...

She cradled his head against her shoulder and stroked his hair. "Oh, Eric..."

He pulled back and took her by the arms. And he looked into her eyes, deeply. For an endless span of time.

She shook herself. Really, she had to clarify things a little. "This doesn't mean—"

"Shh." His finger sealed her lips again. "Explanations are for strangers. We are not strangers. We never were that." She put her hands flat against his chest. She had a thousand things to say. But they all kept flying away. His eyes were so deep. They went down and down forever. "I assume nothing. You needn't fear."

He *did* assume. She could see it there. Shining in his spruce-green eyes.

But—right then, did she care?

Uh-uh.

He was holding her. He wanted her, and, oh, she

did want him, want his hard body against hers, his strong arms around her. For this night, in her cousin's tent, in the camp of the *kvina soldars*.

It was not such an easy thing, this quest of hers. Mostly it seemed she was getting nowhere—except in trouble. And in one sense, he *was* her adversary, keeping from her what she needed to know.

But in another, deeper way she truly did feel bound to him. Beyond being adversaries, they were also comrades. He would fight at her side if it came to that. He would willingly lay down his life for hers.

And as she looked up at him, she knew she would do the same for him.

It *was* a bond between them. A powerful one. Wherever this all might lead in the end, it would be an honest thing, to be with him tonight.

She felt the smile of acceptance curve her lips.

In response he whispered her name. "Brit…"

She took the sides of his shirt and gathered the soft leather, sliding it upward, fingers skimming the firm, hot flesh along his ribs, pulling the shirt over his head and tossing it in the corner with the rest of their things.

His smooth bare chest gleamed in the darkness. And there was the medallion….

The sight of it—of the twining serpent, the four mystic animal faces, the cloverleaf cross at the center—took the shivery, sexual moment and twisted it. Ruined it.

She turned her head away.

He caught her chin, guided her back. "Look. Know. It is there for you when you want it. And only then."

She pushed at his chest—regretfully. But firmly.

He dropped his hands to his sides.

They stared at each other, inches—and now suddenly, miles—apart. They were both breathing heavily.

"I can't do it," she said at last. "It just wouldn't be right."

He cocked an eyebrow at her. "And so, when the warrior women learn I have failed to please you, I die."

Like she could let him get away with that one. "Oh, please. You know that is *so* not going to happen."

"But I must—"

"Please me? That's right. And you have. Thoroughly. End of problem."

"I'd like to do more." He looked so sincere. And so devastatingly sexy. Damn him.

She shrugged, the gesture cool—everything she wasn't inside. "Get over it."

"So much bravado. Strange how it suits you."

"Bravado? This is not bravado. This is me. Trying, against all odds, to get through to *you.*"

"And I have heard you. No more pleasuring. Not tonight."

"Not tonight, not *ever.*"

"Ah," he said, as if he understood. But he didn't. He was absolutely certain tonight had been only the beginning of the *pleasuring* they'd share. He didn't believe for a moment that she meant what she said.

And how could she expect him to? She didn't believe it herself.

She pointed at the pallet where their things were piled. "You can sleep there. I'll take the other one."

"I am yours to command."

Oh, yeah, right. "Go to bed then."

"As you wish, so shall it ever be."

* * *

The hawk dropped from the sky. Its eyes were dragon eyes, burning red. Flames shot from its beak, searing all in its path. She put up her arms to shield her face and a single cry escaped her.

Brit woke sitting up, arms across her eyes. Slowly she lowered them.

The fire was down to a low glow of coals. Her pallet was a mess, the furs and blankets wrinkled and lumped up beneath her.

And Eric was awake, lying on his side, his head propped on a hand...watching her. The medallion hung to the side. His gorgeous chest gleamed at her. His blankets were down to his waist. She'd made a concentrated effort *not* to look as he got ready for bed. And now, she couldn't help but wonder...

If those blankets slipped a little lower, would she get a view of what she'd felt against her belly earlier?

She jerked her gaze—and her thoughts—away from where they had no business going.

His eyes were waiting, way too alert, unsettlingly aware. "Bad dream?"

She grunted. It was answer enough. And then she concentrated on straightening her bedding. At first, she tried to do it without getting up. She only made things worse.

"Allow me to help you with that."

"No, thanks." At least she'd had the sense—unlike *some* people—to keep everything but her boots on when she crawled beneath the blankets. She was showing him nothing as she stumbled to her feet and tugged on the heavy pallet until it was reasonably smooth again.

She was just about to slide back in, where it was warm, when he said with infuriating good humor, "Always such an angry sleeper."

She shot him a look. *Always,* he'd said. That meant he must have watched her sleep, at Asta's house....

"Not angry. Restless." She lifted the covers, got under them and settled them over herself. "Good night." She shut her eyes.

"Brit?"

Outside somewhere an owl asked "Who, who, who," as she considered not responding. But in the end, she gave in and muttered, "What?"

"The blond warrior woman, the one called Rinda..."

"What about her?"

"She called you 'cousin.'"

"Because I am."

He was quiet for a moment. Finally he said, "She looks like you."

Brit stared through the smoke hole above. The night sky was cloudy, a deep grayness, hiding the stars. "She's the image of my mother at twenty-five or so."

Eric made a low noise in his throat. "I have it. Brian the Blackhearted..."

Brit felt a funny little sadness, a heaviness near her heart. "They called my uncle that?"

"They did. And he was."

"Blackhearted..."

"Yes. And was he Rinda's father?"

She could see no reason—beyond a petty desire to goad him—to keep what she knew to herself. "Yes. He raped Ragnild."

"Ah," he said, as if that explained everything. And really, it probably did. "So Ragnild wished to meet you."

"That's right." *She believes that I'll someday be queen,* she thought. But she didn't say it. Many, after all, believed that Eric would one day be king. If Brit were to be queen, then that would mean...

No. Better not even go there. And besides. Since Valbrand lived, *he* would most likely be the next king, once all this confusion got straightened out. No way Valbrand would be marrying his little sister. Even in Gullandria, they weren't into stuff like that.

So much for Ragnild's dreams.

And what, Brit wondered, was Valbrand doing right now?

Really, there was so much she wanted—*needed*—to know. "Eric?"

He made a noise that told her he was listening.

"How old were you when you first met my brother?"

He didn't answer for a moment. But the silence was a musing one. Then he said, "So young, I don't even remember a time when I didn't know him. I was two when he was born. And it seems, in my memory, that he is always there. We played together, from the time he was old enough to crawl. And then, for a while, it was the three of us."

"Kylan, too?"

"Yes. And then Kylan was gone. It was only us two again, your brother and me. From wooden swords to swords of steel. We shared the same teachers, in the classroom, in the training yard. We were bloodbound when I was twelve and he was ten—do you know what it means, to be bloodbound?''

She repeated what she'd read in one of the books she'd found in the palace library about life in Gullandria. "To be bloodbound is to share with another a blood oath of loyalty and commitment. It's an oath that binds equals, makes them brothers in the truest sense—as opposed to bloodsworn, which binds one of lesser rank to a ruler or a leader.''

"You have it right.''

"I wonder...''

"Ask.''

"Well, did Valbrand ever speak of us—of his sisters and his mother, in America?''

There was complete silence, suddenly, as if the night itself held its breath.

"Eric?'' she prompted at last, when she was sure he would never answer.

He said, "It was bad for Valbrand, when your mother left—you three princesses were only babies. He didn't know you. So your loss he could bear. But the loss of a mother... It leaves a ragged hole of longing, a scar that never completely heals. And then, so shortly after that, for him to lose your brother, Kylan, as well...'' Eric's voice trailed off, as if no words could express how terrible that had been. "I was fourteen when my mother died. Valbrand got me through it. Because he *knew*. He understood...'' Eric made a low sound. "And I haven't answered your question, have I?''

Her question seemed unimportant by then. She was thinking how bad it must have been for Valbrand. And for Eric, too. Brit and her mother had issues—but the thought of Ingrid not *being* there. That would be way hard to get through. "It's okay. I can understand why he wasn't thinking much about his baby sisters."

"The truth is, he did think of you. And he spoke of you. More and more often as we came into manhood. He spoke of the time he knew would come someday, when you and your sisters would venture across the sea to visit the land of your birth. He spoke now and then of going to visit you in America. But he never quite got around to it. I think, perhaps, there were traces of bitterness, still, within him—bitterness at your mother, for leaving him, for never coming back."

"Bitterness…" Such a sad word. A word full of *might have been,* of *if I had only,* a word heavy with hurt and regret.

"Only traces." Eric's voice was warm with reassurance. "Nothing that couldn't be healed, given time and tenderness. He wasn't a man to hold grudges, not a man to let bitterness own him. He was bigger… better than that."

Was.

How easily he spoke of her brother in the past tense. Was it shrewdness on his part, to maintain consistency with the original lie?

Or merely the sad truth?

No.

She'd never believe that. She'd *seen* her brother. Valbrand still lived. All Eric Greyfell's clever lies wouldn't steal the truth she knew in her heart.

She rolled to her right side, facing the dying fire— she would have rather faced the shadows, but her sore shoulder wouldn't let her. She stared at the glowing embers until sleep closed her eyes and carried her off into dreams again.

The next morning the clouds had cleared away. The sky was the startling blue of a newborn baby's eyes. They went to Ragnild's tent for an early breakfast of porridge and jerky.

Eric was ordered to wait outside while Ragnild questioned Brit concerning his performance the night before.

"How well did he pleasure you?" Ragnild demanded.

Brit had her answer ready. "He is a lover without peer. I am well satisfied."

Yeah, okay. The well-satisfied part was an outright lie. But from the kisses they'd shared, she felt justified in making the leap to calling him a good lover.

As for the bit about him being without peer? Well, hey. That was one of the great things about Gullandria. You could call a man "without peer" and nobody would think you were being pretentious.

Satisfied with Brit's answer, the camp leader allowed Eric to join them in the tent. Ragnild even granted him permission to sit with the rest of them and share the meal, as though he was more than a mere man, fit only to provide sexual pleasure and children.

After the meal Ragnild had a fine mare—white, the cutest gray boots on her front hooves—brought from the camp's remuda.

"For you, my daughter's cousin," said the leader proudly, stroking the mare's silky forehead. "May she carry you without stumbling, onward to meet your destiny.''

A horse was a very big gift—one that Brit accepted gratefully. A good horse would come in handy during her stay in the Vildelund. Also, having her own horse meant she wouldn't have to share a ride with Eric to get back to the village. They'd travel faster if they each had their own mount—not to mention that she could skip the forced intimacy of having his body pressed against her back for the next six or seven hours, providing a constant reminder of what she'd promised herself she was not going to do with him.

''Thank you, Ragnild. Does this fine horse have a name?''

''Svald.''

''And that means?''

''Why, whatever you would have it mean.''

Brit took the reins.

Rinda handed her three small, hard apples. ''Here, cousin. A few apples always smooth the way between a horse and her new owner.''

Brit offered the apples to Svald. The mare lipped them up and chomped them, then nuzzled for more. Brit stroked her fine, sleek neck and blew in her nostrils.

Eric said he'd help her to mount.

''No, thanks. I can manage.'' She grabbed a handful of braided mane and hoisted herself to the horse's strong back. The muscles of her legs and buttocks complained. But the long soak in the hot spring the night before had helped a lot. The stiffness wasn't as bad as it might have been.

Brit promised to visit again, and she and Eric set out through the trees.

At the top of the first rise, they paused to survey the rugged, tree-covered land before them. Eric said, "You will have trouble finding those women again."

"I know the way."

He smiled. That smile warmed her—intentions to the contrary. "They will move camp now. They're probably packing things up as we speak."

"But why?"

"They live free. They can't allow outsiders to know where to find them."

"They can trust us. We'd never betray them."

"*We?* High praise." He was grinning.

"I never mistrusted you. I know you're an honest man—well, except for that big lie you keep telling me about Valbrand." She put up a hand. "Don't say it. I don't need to hear it—and are you telling me I've found Ragnild and my cousin only to lose them again?"

"You *will* see them, in the future. On that I would wager my best hunting rifle."

"But you just said—"

"That you would have trouble finding them again. I didn't say anything about *them* finding *you*. I'm certain they will, when next they feel a need to seek you out."

They reached the village at a little past three that afternoon. Asta came running out, followed by her daughters-in-law and a chattering knot of children. There were glad cries of greeting and warm hugs all around.

Mist grabbed Brit around the knees and squeezed. "Bwit, I miss you. Miss you, miss you, vewwy much…"

Brit scooped her up and held her close. "Give me a big squeeze. See? I'm right here—and you are so strong!"

The little one was already squirming to get down. Brit let her go with some reluctance, glancing up to see that Eric was watching, looking way too smug.

Oh, right. Back to what a wonderful wife she was going to make. Because she loved kids and would no doubt be yearning to *breed* a passel of them. Yeah, sure. As in, don't hold your breath.

Asta took her arm. "Eric, see to the horses. Brit, come inside immediately. I must check your bandage, and then you are to eat a hearty meal. After the meal no doubt you'll enjoy a trip to the bathhouse. And after that you'll have a long, healing night's rest."

"Sounds terrific," said Brit. "Good food, a bath and some rest." She might as well drop the bombshell now. "I'll need all that to be fresh for the big day tomorrow."

Asta's eyes narrowed. Eric looked bleak.

"Oh," Brit said, with an offhand wave. "Sorry. I've been meaning to tell you. Tomorrow I'm heading for Drakveden Fjord. I want to have a look at what's left of my plane."

Chapter Nine

Asta let out a small cry of outrage. Then she started objecting. "Brit, you'll do no such thing. It isn't safe for you to be wandering all over the Vildelund."

"My safety isn't the issue here. I'm going."

"Of course your safety is the issue. You are the daughter of our king, and your life is precious above all else."

"Asta. There's no sense in arguing about this. I'm heading out tomorrow at first light."

"Eric." Asta was actually wringing her hands. "Talk to her."

Eric looked as if he wouldn't mind strangling someone—and Brit had a good idea who that someone might be. "Take her inside," he commanded. "Feed her. I'll see to the horses. Then she and I will share an evening stroll."

* * *

The "evening stroll" happened an hour later, in waning daylight. And as it turned out, there was no strolling involved. Eric must have decided he didn't want to argue with her on the village street, where anyone might hear them going at each other. So he shooed the others out. They faced off as they had the morning before, alone in Asta's longhouse, on either side of the deal table.

"What is the point of this?" Eric demanded. "You put yourself in harm's way for the mere thrill of it."

"No, I do not. And there *is* a point, since you asked. I want to have a look at that plane."

"To what purpose?"

"I want to see what was done to it, to make it lose oil pressure out of nowhere like that."

"Ah," he sneered. "Not only a licensed pilot, but an airplane mechanic, as well."

"I just want to have a look, okay? I just want to see if I can—"

"No." His voice was carefully controlled—but his expression was thunderous. "It is not, in any way, *okay.*"

"Well, fine. It's not okay. But I'm going, so get used to the idea."

"You will learn nothing. And you might very well get yourself killed."

"So be it. A little danger I can handle. It's way preferable to hanging around here, twiddling my thumbs, getting the brush-off every time I dare to ask a question about my brother." She was leaning toward him, knuckles braced on the table. "Unless…"

He looked bleak. "Tell me."

"Well, I might be willing to change my mind, if you were to decide you're finally ready to trust me. If you'd agree to take me to my brother…"

"How can I do that? Your brother is dead."

"You keep saying that. Why don't I believe it?"

"You don't *want* to believe it."

"That's right. I don't. Because it's not true."

They enjoyed a short, angry stare down.

Brit was the one who looked away. She pushed herself back from the table and stood fully upright, wrapping her arms around herself, turning from him, toward the stove. "I'm sick of it." She tossed the words over her shoulder. "I'm *through* with it. I'm not going to learn anything more staying here."

"Your injury—"

She whirled on him. "Is better. Better every day. Yes, it's still tender. But it's not going to stop me from doing what I need to do. I prevented a rape yesterday. I was slapped to the ground by a big, bossy *kvina soldar*. I rode bareback for hours—yesterday *and* today. My shoulder is no worse for all the activity. Don't you even try to use it as an excuse to keep me here. There is nothing more for me to do here. I've asked all my questions and I've gotten too few answers. I've got to look elsewhere. Otherwise, what's left for me but to return to my father's palace with nothing to show for all I've been through but an ugly burden of guilt over my dead guide and a gross-looking scar from a renegade's poisoned arrow?"

The look of fury had left his face. Now he regarded her with dangerous tenderness. "There could be more than that. There could be—"

"I know where you're going." She was shaking her

head. "Don't." Just because she couldn't stop imagining what it might be like to roll around on the bed furs with him didn't mean she was ready to wear his medallion and bear his children.

When she bound her life to a man, that man was going to respect her as a full equal. And he was *always* going to be able to trust her with the truth.

He was coming around the table toward her. He stopped about three inches away.

She groaned. "Why am I always standing here waiting when you get to me?"

He lifted a hand.

She should have backed away. But as usual, she didn't.

His finger brushed the line of her jaw, leaving delicious little tingles of longing in its wake. "Perhaps you like it, when I'm near you."

She lifted her chin and looked at him dead-on. "Maybe I do. Maybe I wish..." Oh, what was she saying?

"Don't stop now." His voice had gone velvety, lovely, warm.

She pushed his tender hand away and stepped back as she should have a moment before. "Forget all that. What you need to accept right now is that tomorrow I *am* going to have a look at my plane. Short of locking me up and throwing the key away, you're not going to stop me."

He was looking bleak again. "It's more than thirty kilometers from here, over rough, steep terrain. The hazards are endless. You won't only have to worry about the occasional renegade and other fierce bands of *kvina soldars*. There are also large meat-eating animals with sharp claws and long teeth."

"In case you haven't figured it out by now, I've spent my life going to places where the terrain is rugged, the animals predatory and the locals restless. And yet, here I am. In one piece. And ready to go."

He was the one who stepped back then. "There is no stopping you, is there?"

"Finally. You're getting it."

He gave her one of those long, unwavering looks—to let her know he was about to make a point that would not be negotiable. "If you're going, I am going with you."

She smiled then.

He grunted. "So. That was your plan all along."

"Well…"

"What?"

"I have to admit, the idea makes me a little edgy. You know how it is with us…." She let him finish that thought for himself. "I don't need the distraction. However, you know the way and I don't. I can use a good guide, not to mention…"

"What?" he prompted, when she didn't finish.

She shrugged. "You're quick and strong. I have no doubt you know how to handle a weapon. You're a good man to have on my side if I have to fight my way out of a sticky situation."

He didn't look happy, exactly. But he definitely looked a little less fed up. "Let us hope for good weather, for an absence of 'sticky situations.'"

"Hope for the best, be ready for the worst. It's the only way to go, if you ask me."

* * *

They set out at six the next morning, before the sun crested the hills to the east. Asta had loaned Brit a saddle. She stood outside to tell them goodbye.

"Bad weather coming," she warned, as they mounted the horses. "If you must go, then leave on the morrow."

"Oh, Asta." Brit stroked the side of Svald's sleek neck. "Come on. There's not a cloud in the sky."

Eric, on a muscular gelding, gestured at the barometer beside the front door. "Falling fast." Brit only looked at him. He turned to his aunt. "It appears the coming storm will not stop us. We are going today."

Asta's frown deepened, but she said no more. She stood out in the street and waved as they rode away. Pure foolishness, she'd called the venture the night before, when she returned to her house to learn that Eric had failed to talk Brit out of going. An idiot's quest.

To a certain degree, Brit had to agree with her. But she wasn't going to learn a damn thing sitting around the Mystic village, being coddled by Asta and the other women, getting no answers to her questions, daydreaming too much about Eric while she plucked the occasional game bird and helped Sif with the wash.

And wait another day in case the weather turned bad? No, thanks. A little rain wasn't going to slow her down. And, anyway, it was warmer than it had been. Felt like in the low forties already. A much more pleasant temperature for traveling than yesterday or the day before.

She felt eager. Ready. Felt…a sort of happy shiver running beneath her skin to think that they were on the way.

She glanced at the man on the gelding beside her. Taking her daydreams right along with her. Oh, yes, she was. Hey. Couldn't be helped. A girl's gotta do what a girl's gotta do. She needed a guide, and he knew his way around the Vildelund.

They rode with the rising sun at their backs until they reached the forest that rimmed the village and its fields. About a mile into the deep, cold shadows of the tall trees, the trail came to a three-way fork. Eric laid his reins to the gelding's neck and the horse, bridle wise, took the right fork, to the north. Brit followed his lead.

At first the horses jogged easily on level ground, the trail wide enough that they could ride side by side. But soon enough they began climbing. The trail narrowed and Brit fell in at the rear. Above, through the lacy branches of the trees, clouds gathered. The wind was rising.

For a couple of hours it was much the same kind of travel as the day before and the day before that—up and down the sides of steep hills, on trails that led them in zigzagging switchbacks—much the same, only darker and windier.

They had just reached the base of a hill when Eric reined in and put up a hand. Quietly he slid to the ground. Brit followed his lead. He indicated a clump of black boulders faintly visible through the trees, perhaps fifteen feet from the trail. He took his horse by the bridle. Brit did the same.

They moved cautiously into the trees. When they reached the black rocks, Eric signaled her in close. They held the muzzles of the horses and were silent. Waiting.

Eric tipped his head, gesturing at a gap in the high, sloping rocks. Two quiet steps to the side and she could peer through.

She saw four men—young, on foot, three armed with crossbows, dagger hilts visible in sheaths tied at the thigh. The third had a rifle. Two carried a rough pole between them; a slain doe, gutted, was tied to it, dangling.

"Renegades?" She mouthed the word, careful to make no sound.

"Perhaps," he mouthed in answer.

She understood. No percentage in finding out. Better to just keep their heads down and their mounts quiet until the potential threat could pass on by.

The wind rushed down the canyon, keening. Svald shifted, nervous, ready to dance. Brit laid her face to the silky muzzle and whispered very low. "Shh. Easy, my darling, easy my sweet girl." The mare quieted.

They waited some more, as the wind whipped around them, singing eerily through the trees. Lightning flashed and booming thunder followed. The first drops of rain began to fall. Finally, after the four men were long gone, Eric led her around the stand of boulders and onto the trail where the men had passed.

"How did you know they were there?" she asked before they mounted up again.

He shook his head as lightning blazed in the sky above. Thunder boomed and rolled away. "Later. Now we must move on." They mounted and went in the opposite direction from the four men.

They covered what was left of the ravine floor quickly and within minutes they were climbing again. The wind tore at them, lightning speared the sky, angry thunder booming in its wake. The sky opened up and the rain poured down—fat drops, coming harder and faster.

They fought their way upward as the downpour intensified. In no time the trail was awash in mud. The mud turned to rivulets, then to small, rushing streams.

"We must leave the trail. It will soon be a river," Eric called over his shoulder, shouting against the wind.

Brit followed him into the trees, her head low against the mare's neck, smelling rain and wet horse, her beanie and the hair beneath it plastered to her skull.

Eric led her on, through the close-growing evergreens. More than once she got whacked by low-hanging branches. And even there, in the thickness of the trees, the rain got through, whipping at their faces, driven by the relentless wind. Svald, bless her sweet heart, was a surefooted animal. They picked their way along the steep slope of the hill, moving east now, climbing as they went.

They were practically upon the mouth of the cave before she saw it: two shelves of rock surrounded by trees, a tall, dark hole between. Eric dismounted and climbed the rest of the way on foot, leading the gelding, slipping a little on the soggy ground, but jumping at last to the lower shelf at the cave's entrance and urging the gelding up after him. There was space on the ledge for him, his horse, Brit and Svald, with room to spare.

He waved her on. She slid from the saddle and followed, leading her horse, landing on her feet at the cave's entrance, Svald scrambling a little, but ending up at her side.

"Stay here." Eric handed her the gelding's reins and vanished into the darkness. Brit surprised herself by letting him go without a word of protest. Truth to tell, she thought as she stood there in the mouth of the cave, dripping wet and shivering with cold, she was feeling more than a little discouraged with herself. Concerning the weather, Asta had been all too right. Maybe she should have listened.

But she'd always been that way. When she was ready to go, there was just no stopping her. A character flaw? Well, yeah. In some circumstances.

Like, for instance, this one.

The horses shook the heavy, soaked braids of their manes, flinging icy water everywhere, including on her. Beyond the ledge, the rain was turning slushy—a snow and rain mix.

Terrific. Perfect. Wonderful. Would they end up snowed in here, thanks to her pigheadedness?

Now, wouldn't that be lovely? Way to go, Brit.

"This way," Eric said from behind her. He stood about fifteen feet into the cave. He was carrying...a flaming torch?

"Where did you get that?"

"It's always wise to keep safe places, stocked and ready, for times like this one. We're fortunate. No scavengers have found this cave since last I was here." Really, the guy never ceased to amaze her. "Come," he said.

She went, leading the horses into the darkness, toward the tall, proud man with the blazing light.

Chapter Ten

The cave was a tunnel for about a hundred feet. Then it opened to a wide, shadowy chamber. Eric went directly to the circle of stones at the center. Within the circle a fire was laid and waiting to be lit.

He lowered the torch to the kindling and the fire caught. The smoke spiraled up and disappeared into the shadows above. Apparently, there were gaps in the rocks up there, a natural flue that let the smoke escape.

Brit swiped off her wet beanie, dropped it to a nearby rock and raked her fingers back through her hair. Ugh. Dripping and tangled. She really should have taken a moment, back there when it started raining, to unzip her collar and make use of the waterproof hood built into her jacket.

Eric stuck the torch into the dirt. He turned it until the flame went out, then dropped the heavy stick beside the ring of stones. He glanced up to find her staring at him and returned the favor with a dead-on kind of look.

Well, okay, she thought, shrugging and raising her hands, palms out. All my fault we're here. Message received. My bad.

He didn't seem particularly mollified by her show of meekness.

So fine, she thought. Be that way.

She shifted her glance to the licking, rising flames of the fire and her low spirits lifted a fraction—at the brightness and warmth and the cheery crackling sounds it made. She took a look around. Gleaming in the far shadows, near another tunnel opposite the one they had come through, she could see a small pool.

"A spring?" she asked, and then wished she hadn't. He probably wouldn't even bother to answer.

But he did. "The water is clear, very cold—and safe to drink." He took the reins of his horse from her. "We must see to our mounts." There were supplies stacked on a ledge of rock near the cave wall: a pile of blankets, a bag of oats, a bucket....

From his saddlebag Eric produced a brush and a curry comb. "Put your pistol aside."

She did as he instructed, removing her coat so she could take off her shoulder holster, setting the gun and the holster on a flat-topped rock a few feet from the fire. She was shivering, so she put her coat back on.

They unsaddled, wiped down and brushed the long-haired horses, unbraiding and combing out their manes so they would dry. It took a while. They had to share the comb and brush. Midway through, no longer cold, she took off her coat and set it on a rock, the outside spread toward the fire to dry.

They were silent as they worked. Eric wore a grim look the whole time. Did she blame him?

Not really.

"I'll feed the horses," he said when the job of getting the animals dry and groomed was done. "Take off your wet clothes. Lay them out to dry." He tossed her a blanket to wrap herself in.

Her socks were dry, thanks to her heavy boots. But upward from there to her waist she was wet to the skin.

On top, the news was better. Her water-repellent jacket, though damp on the outside, had protected her underneath. Water had gotten in around her neck, but not a lot. It would dry quickly if she stood near the fire.

Her bandage was fine. Hooray for small favors.

She retreated to a corner of the cave, where she took off her boots and then hopped around in her socks, getting off the clammy jeans and thermal pants. Eric never glanced her way—or if he did, she didn't catch him at it.

Yeah, okay. It was kind of childish, to keep darting suspicious looks his way to make sure he wasn't peeking. As if it mattered if he watched her hopping around without her jeans on. He wouldn't have seen much, anyway—just her looking seriously awkward, with bare legs. And given his current mood, why would he bother?

She wrapped her lower body in the blanket, put her boots back on and hobbled to the fire carrying her two sets of soggy pants. Once she'd spread the clothes on the rocks several feet from the flames, where they could soak up the heat without getting singed, she got her comb from her saddlebag and perched on a rock to work the tangles from her hair.

About then Eric finished with the horses and withdrew to a corner of his own to hop around getting out of his wet things—not that she watched him. Of course she didn't. She just knew what the procedure entailed, having done it herself a few minutes ago.

Soon enough, a blanket tied at his waist, he joined her at the fire. He was bare-chested. His thick shearling jacket didn't have a zipper. Water must have gotten through...

She realized she was staring at him again—and no, not at the medallion, though it gleamed against his skin. She was looking at his beautiful, muscular, smooth chest.

She blinked, jerked her glance downward and regarded her boots as she yanked at the tangles in her hair.

He chuckled.

She looked up, glaring, sharp words rising to her lips.

"You have something to say?" His eyes were gleaming.

She cleared her throat. "Uh, no. Not a thing."

Really, why rag on him? She was *grateful* to him, she truly was. If she'd been on her own, she'd have ridden right up on those four mean-looking characters with that poor dead doe. And even if she'd somehow gotten past them, she'd be out in the rain right now, soaked to the skin, wondering what to do next—instead of safe in a warm, dry place, reasonably comfortable while she waited out the storm.

"Well," she said cautiously, daring to hope they might manage to be on good terms while they were stuck here. "I guess you're not *that* mad at me."

He was laying his clothes on the rocks, the lean, strong muscles of his arms and shoulders bunching and releasing as he worked. He sent her a glance.

She realized she was doing it again—staring at his body. She jerked her gaze downward.

"A fine pair of boots you have there."

She couldn't help smiling. "I like 'em." She lifted her head. His eyes were waiting. "So. We're okay then—I mean, you and me? You're not totally furious with me for getting us into this jam?"

He seemed to consider, then replied. "I confess, I was angry. But while you were looking at your boots, it occurred to me that I might as well blame the rain for falling as be angry at you for going where you think you have to go." He half sat on a steeply sloping rock.

She worked a final stubborn knot from a damp lock of hair. "I don't just *think* I have to go there." He only looked at her. She read his expression and couldn't help grinning. "Determined to avoid an argument, are we?"

"I am trying with all my might."

The knot came free. "I can see that. And I've got to say you're doing an excellent job."

They had jerky in their saddlebags and dried apples and grain bars—pressed oats and nuts, sweetened with honey. They spread blankets on the floor and sat down for lunch, using their saddles for backrests.

Brit had two sticks of jerky, several dried apple slices, a grain bar and a precious bag of M&Ms laid out on a handkerchief at her side. She took one of the jerky sticks. "So now can you tell me how you knew those men were on the trail?"

He was chewing on a bite of grain bar. He swallowed. "The truth is, I don't *know* how I knew. They might have made a noise that I heard somewhere below the threshold of my conscious mind. Or maybe it was the quality of the silence."

Silence? The wind had been blowing, making the tree branches sway and sigh. And what about the jingle of their bridles, the soft clop-clop of the horses' hooves?

He must have seen by her expression that she didn't understand. "It's…an instinct, I suppose. An instinct one develops, over time. When we pass through the forest, the smaller creatures—all but the foolish squirrels and some of the cheekier birds—go quiet, wary of us as potential predators. Though there is the noise of our passing, there is also a circle of silence around us as we move. When those men got too close, they brought their own circle with them. I sensed it."

She gestured with her piece of jerky. "Ah. Well. Now, that explains it."

"You still do not follow?"

She stared into his eyes for a moment. "Yes. I follow, at least to a degree…"

He tore off a bite of jerky and so did she. They both chewed. Great thing about dried meat—really kept the old jaw muscles in top form.

She swallowed. "So you've spent a lot of time here, in the Vildelund, over the years?"

"I have."

"Your father brought you?"

He shook his head. "My father had his work at the king's side in the south, demanding work that left few opportunities for family trips. But my mother loved the Mystic life. She would come often to the Vildelund for lengthy visits. Much of the time I would come with her."

She thought of her brother and wondered. Sif had said he used to come here. "And Valbrand? Did he come, too?" He sent her a look. She bristled. "What? Now I can't even ask you about him? We talked about him the other night."

He considered for a moment, then granted, "That we did."

She set down her half-eaten grain bar. "I just want to…know about him. Please. It means a lot—to hear how he felt about things, about how he was." She used the past tense without the slightest hesitation, though she didn't for a minute believe her brother was really dead. It only seemed to her the best way to show Eric that, right now at least, she wasn't leading him anywhere, wasn't trying to trip him up. She was only a sister longing to learn about the brother she had never had the opportunity to know. She asked again, "Did Valbrand used to come to the Vildelund with you?"

And he answered. "Yes. Many times."

"Did he like it here?"

"He did."

"Why?"

"He liked the wildness of the land, I think, the peace that can be found in living simply."

"The same things you like."

"Yes."

"He didn't think much of the life at court, then?"

A ghost of a smile haunted Eric's fine mouth. "Ah, but he did. He loved the life at court."

She made a small sound in her throat. "Well. Easy to please, wasn't he?"

"You could say that, I suppose. Valbrand had a talent for living within each moment. Wherever he was, he never wished himself elsewhere. He always seemed to enjoy himself at functions of state. No matter how long or tedious the event, he would be alert and smiling, thoroughly engrossed." Eric stared into the fire as though looking into a kinder past. "That was your brother. Always interested. And seeing the good first, in every man."

Though it was off the all-important subject of her brother, she couldn't stop herself from asking, "And what about you? Do you enjoy the life at Isenhalla?"

"Not as much as Valbrand did." They shared a glance. He added, "But I do find it stimulating. After all, His Majesty and my father are responsible, to some extent, for the well-being of every Gullandrian. It's important work that they do. I grew to manhood knowing that the time would come when I would step forward to assume the sacred duty of helping my king— your brother—to rule this land. I was content in that knowledge. I was committed to preparing myself fully for the future I knew awaited me."

"And now?"

His mouth had a rueful curl to it. "Now I would

say that I no longer see my future as a clear, straight road before me. There are twists and turns, corners I cannot see around.''

''You mean, since my brother was lost at sea?''

He studied her face for a moment, his eyes narrowed. And then he stuck out his right arm, wrist up. She saw the white ridge of scar tissue. He said, ''Valbrand had a scar to match this one.''

''From when you were bloodbound to each other?''

He nodded. ''In the bloodbinding ceremony, each of us was bled—a copious bleeding, believe me—into the same deep bowl. Then, our wounds still open, we took turns, the blood running free down our arms, passing the bowl back and forth, drinking our mingled blood until every drop was gone.'' He let his arm fall to his side. ''So I have drunk your brother's blood—as he drank mine. When he was lost, I lost not only my dearest friend and bloodbound brother, but also my future partner in the work of ruling this land. It was a terrible blow, a cleaving at the center of who I am. As if half of my true self was slashed away.''

She didn't know what to say, so she said nothing, only reached out and brushed her fingers down the side of his arm in a wordless acknowledgment of his loss. Though she remained certain Valbrand had returned, she had no doubt Eric had once believed him dead—and that that belief had changed him in a deep, irrevocable way.

Eric caught her hand, clasped it briefly, then let it go.

She felt a warmth all through her. A closeness to him that had nothing to do with desire. This was something else. It was what she'd sensed between them two nights ago, in Rinda's tent in the camp of the *kvina soldars*.

The closeness of comrades…

There was wood—maybe half a cord—stacked near the supplies against the cave wall. And a much smaller pile of logs nearer the fire. He rose with surprising grace, given the way the blanket was wrapped so close around his legs, and got a fresh log from the smaller pile. He crouched to add it to the flames.

She let herself admire the fine, strong shape of his back, the play of light and shadow on the bumps of his spine, the healthy bloom on his smooth skin as he positioned the log in the fire. A few winking sparks shot up, weaving toward the darkness above for a brave, soaring moment, then surrendering to gravity and gently showering back down.

He returned to the blanket and got comfortable against his saddle. "And what of you, oh fearless one? To whom are you bound?"

She rolled her eyes. "Fearless. Right." She met his eyes. "No, really. I'm far from fearless."

"Yet you never let your fear rule you."

"That's right. Hey. Talk to my mother. She claims I actually seek out the things that scare me."

"And you would do this because…?"

"Well, my mother would say, for the dangerous thrill of confronting my own fear."

"And does your mother have it right?"

She sighed. "Maybe. Sometimes. I've always felt…out of place, I guess. As if I'm looking for something and it's never there." She swallowed, though her mouth was empty.

He asked, his voice gentle, "What things truly frighten you?"

She thought for a moment. "Oh, dying. Original, huh? I guess I'm like most people—not up for that yet."

"Yet you could face it. You *have* faced it. Recently."

Her hand went automatically to her shoulder. He nodded and she found herself nodding in response.

He said, "You will face death again, there is no escaping that."

"Yeah. But I'd seriously prefer if I didn't have to do it anytime soon."

"Your mother might say otherwise."

"She would *definitely* say otherwise."

"Mothers can be so irritating—they are too often right."

She made a humphing sound. "Unfortunately."

He shrugged. "The time will come, for all of us, when death will win the day. Our forefathers understood this. They asked only for the chance to die fighting."

Our forefathers. If she closed her eyes, she could almost see them. The bold Norsemen of old in their serpent-thin ships, brutal men bound only by their warrior code, eyes on the far horizon, rowing hard and steady toward the next settled, prosperous, ripe-for-the-picking coastal town.

Eric said, "Death is the one constant, the thing to which we all ultimately surrender, even as we spend our lives denying that death will have us in the end."

What was there to say to that? Nothing—which was exactly what she said.

He asked, "And my original question—to whom are you bound?"

That was a fairly easy one. "My family. My mother, my sisters. My father. Strange. I never knew him for all those years. But the moment I met him, I felt that I'd known him all of my life." She glanced away. She was thinking that she felt the same way about the man who sat beside her. But she didn't want to say it. It would be way unwise, given the circumstances—the two of them, alone by the fire until the storm passed, wearing blankets instead of their clothes.

"Who else?" he prompted.

She did look at him then, chin high, defiant. "My brother." It came out sounding like a taunt.

He didn't rise to the bait. "And…?"

One more person came to mind. "A friend. She lives in Los Angeles. Her name is Dulcie Samples. I met her at a writers' workshop. She has red hair and honest hazel eyes and the biggest heart in California."

"A friend and a true one."

"You got it."

"A friend found at…a writers' workshop?"

"That's right."

"You are an author?"

"Wannabe."

"Wanna—"

"Want to be," she clarified. "I've started ten novels. Haven't finished a one."

"You say that with such bravado. Why?"

"I didn't finish college, either. Some have remarked that there seems to be a pattern here."

If there was a pattern, Eric didn't seem particularly

concerned about it. He asked, "And your friend, Dulcie?"

"She's written three, I think—all the way through to the end. Hasn't sold one yet, but I really believe, for her, that day will come."

"For her—yet not for you?"

She waved a hand. "I gotta be honest. All that sitting, I just can't stick with it."

"A woman of action."

"Well, yeah. I guess so." A few feet away, Svald shook her head and snorted. "See? I get no respect. Not even from my horse."

"I respect you." He was looking at her teasingly, but it didn't matter. She knew he meant what he said. His expression changed, turned more serious. "And what about men? Other than your father...and your brother. Is there a man to whom you feel bound?"

"Not...at the moment." Was that a lie? Maybe. Maybe she did feel bound. Just a little bit—to Eric.

Did he sense she felt that way? If he did, he let it pass. "But there have been men you have...cared for?"

Was this somewhere they ought to be going? Probably not. Still, she heard herself answering, "A few. Somehow, it just never seemed to work out."

"Good," he said.

She couldn't resist. "Fair's fair. What about you?"

"A dalliance or two. Foolish. Long over. For the past seven years, I've been waiting for you."

Oops. No doubt about it now. Time to change the subject.

But she didn't. "Eric. Come on..."

His grin was slow and lazy. "Lead the way."

"Oh, puh-lease. Seven years is pretty close to a decade—and you're how old?"

"I am thirty."

"That's...wild."

"No. It is simply the truth."

"I gotta ask, when you say you were waiting for *me,* you don't really mean me, specifically?"

"That is exactly what I meant. You. Specifically."

"Get outta town."

"Since we are not *in* town, I will assume that is simply one of your American expressions."

"Good thinking. But seriously, at the age of twenty-three, you suddenly decided, 'Hey, enough of this dallying. I'm waiting for Brit.' Is that what you're telling me?"

"Ah. I understand your question now. The truth is that I was waiting for you, specifically. But I didn't know who you would be until you came here, to the Vildelund, in search of me. Until I saw that you wore my medallion."

She found she was staring at his chest again. Staring at the medallion, she told herself.

Yeah, right.

Their saddles almost touched. It was way too easy for him to slide over next to her. He cupped the back of her neck, his warm fingers gliding up into her almost-dry hair.

She gulped. "Get back to your own saddle."

He whispered, "You say that with no conviction."

Well, and how was she supposed to say *anything* with conviction? When his warm, strong body was brushing against hers, when the scent of him was all around her, when she gloried in the feel of his fingers in her hair. "This is *so* not fair…"

"Ah, but it *is* fair. It is fair and right. And exactly as it was meant to be."

"Can we just stay away from the meant-to-bes?"

One sable eyebrow lifted. "If you insist. For now." His fingers stroked down through her hair.

She whispered, suddenly breathless, "When you get so close like this…"

"Yes?"

"I can't…"

"What?"

"Damn you, you'd better just go ahead and kiss me."

"As you wish, so shall it be." He said that—and then that tempting mouth of his stayed right where it was. The medallion was touching her, the weight of it pressing through her sweater and her shirt, to a spot right above her breast.

The other night, in Rinda's tent, the sight of that medallion had been enough to make her put a stop to the magic between them.

Not tonight, though.

Tonight she felt the warm weight of it and it was good. Right.

The only problem? His mouth was three whole inches away.

She slid her hand around his neck. It took just one small tug and—at last—his lips met hers.

Chapter Eleven

A kiss.

His kiss.

How did he do it? He kissed her as if he would never kiss another. As if this kiss was the only kiss that had ever been.

Or would ever be.

The thing was, when he kissed her, she could almost believe that "meant to be" was exactly right. Exactly what they were, the two of them.

Meant to be. And together at last. After all the long, lonely years spent waiting. For this moment.

For all their moments to come....

When he kissed her, she could almost forget her quest to bring her brother home, almost accept his lie that Valbrand was no more. When he kissed her she heard violins, saw sparks leaping, showering down.

When he kissed her, she was certain that this man and this kiss would last forevermore...

He lifted his head, just a little, enough that he could look down at her.

Oh, his eyes...

Nobody had eyes like that. Eyes the color of spruce. Or maybe jade. Eyes that looked into hers so deeply.

Way, way deep. Deeper than anyone had dared—or even cared—to look before.

"Come back here, please," she whispered. "Kiss me some more...."

He answered by again lowering his mouth to hers.

She held his mouth with hers and she slipped a hand up, her fingers brushing the medallion.

Oh, the wonderful smooth, hard skin of his chest, so marvelous to touch. The *heat* of him. She laid her palm flat against his left breast—there. She felt it. The strong, steady beat of his heart.

It was glorious. Impossible. Right.

She could feel how he wanted her—in the way his tender hands stroked her nape and caressed her shoulders, in the needful rhythm of his heartbeat, in the hardness that was pressed against her thigh.

He pulled back again.

She frowned at him. "Don't do that."

"What?"

"Don't pull back."

He bent close again—but only for a fleeting moment, only long enough to quickly brush his lips across hers. Then again he pulled away. He shook his head. Slowly. "I regret that now is not the time."

She felt a stab of irritation. "Night before last you

didn't say that. Night before last you thought it was very much *the time.*''

He retreated to his own saddle.

She sat up. "Okay, what's going on? What did I *do?*''

"Nothing. I could kiss you forever...."

She wrinkled her nose at him. "Well, hey. That clarifies it for me."

He found a twig on the blanket, tossed it into the fire. They watched the flames lick around it, claim it, consume it.

Finally he said, "The other night, I knew you wouldn't have me. I knew you weren't ready. But you would give me kisses. A few sweet embraces. So I took them. I understood that in the end you would push me away. Tonight...I don't want you to do what you might later regret.''

She really wanted to argue. But that was only pure pettiness talking. What he said was the truth. She wasn't ready to get naked with him.

And she might never be. Certainly she wouldn't be until he told her the truth that mattered most—the truth that, for whatever reason, he kept choosing to deny her.

She settled back against her saddle with a sigh. "So, how long do you figure we're going to be stuck here?''

"Until the storm plays out. Tomorrow, at the earliest. That would be my guess.''

She looked at her watch. Barely noon. Whoopee. "Got a deck of cards with you?''

"I regret to say I don't.''

"So, then. What shall we talk about now?''

"Is it necessary that we talk?''

"Not in the least." However, at that moment silence seemed a bad choice. She slanted him a look. "Read any good books lately?"

He played along. "A few. I recently finished Hawking's *A Brief History of Time*."

"No kidding. I didn't know anyone had actually read that one."

"Black holes. Fascinating."

"Oh, yeah, I'd imagine. What about music?"

He put up a hand. "Your turn."

"Okay. Eminem."

"Isn't that a candy?"

"No. I mean the rapper." She fully expected him to think she'd said *wrapper*.

But he surprised her. "Ah, rap—talking in rhythm to music. So distinctly American. And I remember. This rapper you mention spells Eminem phonetically. But it means 'M and M,' for his full name, which is Marshall Mathers."

"Hey. Right on the money."

Eric was frowning. "This Eminem is controversial. I have heard his songs are disrespectful to women—and yet he's a favorite of yours?"

She shrugged. "He's got a bad attitude and problems with his mother. Let's just say I can relate." She picked up the bag of candy beside her, tore off the top and held it his way. "M&M?"

"I believe I will, thank you."

"Go ahead, take five or six."

"I see you are feeling generous."

"Yes, I am."

He looked right at her. "I'd rather have them one

at a time." He grinned at her nod of approval and popped the candy into his mouth.

She took one for herself. They sat back on their saddles and stared into the fire. Sucking. Slowly.

The sound was very faint. It came from the far tunnel, beyond the gleaming underground pool. A sound like a pebble tossed against a rock. Eric recognized it for the signal it was.

Careful to be absolutely silent, he pushed back the blanket beneath which, but for his boots, he was fully dressed. Their clothes had dried by midafternoon. They'd wasted no time in putting them on. For both of them, too much bare skin presented way too much temptation.

His boots waited where he'd left them, near his bedding. He reached for them, pulled them on and tied up the laces.

The fire had burned low. Quietly he rose, got more wood and set the heavy logs gently on the glowing coals. There was rustling behind him, followed by a long, soft sigh. And then a groan. He turned from the fire to look at his woman.

She lay on her back, both arms flung out on the blanket beneath her spread bedroll. Her tangled pale hair fell across the down coat she had used for a pillow. She was scowling. "Ugh," she grumbled. And then she smiled.

He felt his own smile taking form from hers. She slept as she did everything else. Restlessly. With enthusiasm.

Her foot in its heavy wool sock appeared from beneath the covers. She grumbled some more, gave a kick—and her slim denim-clad leg was exposed all the way to the thigh. He resisted the urge to go to her and straighten her blankets, to cover her again. The logs behind him were already catching. If she was chilly now, the freshly stoked fire would warm her soon enough.

He waited, watching to see if she might wake. Though she constantly mumbled and sighed and tossed and turned, after a time he became certain she was deeply asleep.

Only then did he dare to snatch his coat from the rock where he'd left it and move stealthily past her, donning the coat as he went. He crossed the dirt floor of the cavern, went past the small pool formed from an underground spring and on into the pitch black of the far tunnel.

He didn't need light. He knew the way. The tunnel first took him deeper into the hillside. But then, about twenty meters along, it turned sharply to the right.

Within minutes of leaving Brit by the fire, he emerged from the tunnel onto a ledge quite similar to the one through which they'd first entered the cave.

The storm was over, the still night air bracing. His breath came out as mist. The rain had become snow at some point. But it must have stayed a slushy mix almost through to the end; the ground was white, but not to any depth. It wouldn't last. Tomorrow, if the sun came out, the thin layer of snow would melt away to nothing by noon.

In the hush, the trees made faint crackling noises. He waited, every sense attuned.

There he heard it: the slightest movement on the hillside, above him to the left, the sound so small it might have been only the scrabbling of some foolish night-foraging squirrel.

But the sound, Eric knew, was intentional. And not made by a squirrel.

It was made by something much larger, something that walked on two legs, a creature feared throughout the Vildelund by youthful renegades—by all men of flawed character and evil intent.

Eric turned. Saw.

Deep in shadow, beneath the thick branches of a spruce tree, invisible to anyone who didn't know what to look for: black boots.

The boots were attached to a pair of black-clad legs. At about hip height, the rest of the dark figure melted into the tree.

Eric cupped his hands around his mouth and blew. The sound was part whistle, part an echo of wind in the trees. It was their signal from when they were boys.

It meant all clear—no need to hide.

At the signal, Valbrand ducked free of the sheltering tree branches. Sure-footed as a mountain cat, he descended, moving sideways for easy balance, jumping at last to Eric's side at the mouth of the cave.

Chapter Twelve

The black leather mask had been stitched by Asta's talented hands. The seams were almost invisible. It fit the ravaged face beneath like a second skin, the holes at the eyes carefully crafted to a catlike slant.

At the mouth there was little more than a slit. Valbrand's voice came out low, slightly muffled, on a thin cloud of mist. "You are certain she won't wake?"

Eric almost smiled. "As certain as one can be about anything that concerns your contrary youngest sister."

Dark eyes gleamed behind the mask. "I think you are positive now of one thing—that she is yours."

Eric lost the urge to smile. "She knows the truth. Though I tell your lie for you at every turn, she remains certain that she saw you—at the crash site, and in my aunt's longhouse. Nothing will shake her belief."

Valbrand backed away a step. "Must you look at me like that? Yes, I should have heeded your warning and worn the mask when she was so ill. But I was confident that she wouldn't recall what she'd seen."

Eric couldn't let that pass. "Why take such a chance? Unless, in some part of your heart, you *wanted* her to see you—to know that you still live."

The dark gaze shifted away. "The answer is no."

Eric cast his own glance upward toward the star-scattered sky. Somewhere out there in the limitless night, black holes waited to suck down unknowing universes into swirling oblivion. Sometimes he felt it was the same here on earth.

He wondered at his own choices. He had been born to follow the man who stood beside him, conditioned all the years of his life to forge onward at all cost toward a shared central goal: Valbrand would be king, Eric his grand counselor. One to lead and one to provide balance and the objective view, as it was with their fathers before them.

Could the goal ever be realized now? More and more, Eric doubted.

He looked at the dark figure beside him. "Did I ask?"

"You were coming to it."

Denials would be useless. They knew each other too well. "Yes. I grow impatient. Can you blame me?"

"Blame *you?*" Valbrand's voice was gentle, heavy with regret. "Never."

"Then when will you show yourself to her?"

"I cannot say."

The same answer. Always. For too long now, Eric

had dared to hope that his friend would eventually recover from the damage inflicted on him.

But like sand in an hourglass, hope was running out.

It was six months since he had at last found Valbrand, a haunted shell of the man he had been, living in a cave on a tiny island off the coast of Iceland, whispered about by the local fisherman—rough and independent men who knew the old Norse ways.

At first Valbrand would not even emerge from the shadows of the cave to speak with him. Slowly, over long weeks, as one might build trust in an injured wild animal, with gifts of food and blankets to lure the wild man ever nearer, Eric had broken through enough that Valbrand allowed him close.

Weeks more were spent in rebuilding the old trust, in convincing Valbrand to come home. The price? Eric's vow to stay near him and keep the secret that he lived. Until Valbrand declared himself ready, only a chosen few—Mystics all—would know that he survived.

Eric had made the trip south to Isenhalla after leaving his friend—only briefly, Valbrand made him swear—safe with Asta. There, at the silver slate palace of Gullandrian kings, Eric had lied—to his father and to his king. He said his time of seeking was over; he'd at last come to accept the fact that Valbrand was no more. The lie had chafed him from the first, but never so much as now when that lie stood, unbreachable as a mile-high fortress wall, between him and the woman destined to be his.

Valbrand spoke then. "I have been again to the crash site." They had agreed the night before that Valbrand would go.

"And?"

"Men still guard it—six of them, NIB." During Brit's illness, they had returned to the crash site together. They'd spotted the guards, who had come through the fjord by boat. "The boat remains moored three kilometers west of the site. While I watched, they had two with the boat and four on the site. Then the two on the boat went out to relieve two of the men near the plane."

"You're certain now—that they're NIB?"

Valbrand nodded. "I slipped aboard the boat during the brief time it waited empty and stole a quick look around."

"The king's men, then?"

"At least in appearance."

"You don't trust them."

"I trust no one but you. You know that. And I wonder. Surely my father must have sent a mechanic to examine the wreckage. That would be routine procedure. What did that mechanic report?"

The question was purely rhetorical. They could not know what the king might have learned without asking him. And Eric couldn't ask His Majesty such a question, as King Osrik would only become suspicious of his claim that he was certain the crash had been an accident.

Any suspicions on King Osrik's part were dangerous until Valbrand declared himself ready to set aside the mask.

Valbrand said, "What of your plans for the morrow?"

"We go on, to the plane."

The eyes behind the mask narrowed. "Are you mad? She can't be allowed there."

"Your sister cares not what she is allowed. She won't be stopped."

"I thought your plan was to—"

"She has a compass and knows how to use it. She has an accurate map drawn by my father. If I lead her on a fool's chase, she'll only find the way herself in the end."

"Then you must make her understand that the danger is too great. She must go back."

With considerable effort, Eric schooled his voice to a patient tone. "You are the one who refuses to understand. Her way is set. She won't return to the safety of the village until she's examined for herself the wreckage of her plane."

Valbrand shook his head. "There's nothing to be gained by that. Even if the men who guard it turn out to be friendly and go so far as to allow her access, she will find nothing of use."

"Why are we discussing this?" Eric found it ever more challenging to keep the irritation from his voice. "You seek to convince me of what I already know. Perhaps *you* would like to try persuading her?"

A low sound came from behind the mask. "Sarcasm, my friend?"

"Born of frustration. She must be told that you live. Our fathers must know, as well. We tread water while all our hopes drown."

Valbrand chopped the air with a black-gloved hand. "I cannot. Not yet."

"You can. You *choose* not to." Eric leaned closer to the man beside him and spoke lower, with greater intensity. "Don't imagine I think it will be an easy thing. I know that for you to stand bare-faced before your father the king and the eyes of the court will be, in its way, a greater feat than surviving the horror that has already been done to you. I *have* been patient. I have waited on your readiness, by your side as I promised. But there is so much to do. Traitors to expose. Wrongs to make right. None of that will be accomplished while you hide behind a mask."

Valbrand's gaze had shifted away again. "This mask has served me—and our people—well. I have saved lives wearing it."

There was truth in those words. At first, when Valbrand had laid claim to Starkavin, the rare black horse he'd taken from renegades, when he'd asked that Asta create for him a black leather mask and clothing to match it, Eric had been heartened. It had seemed a first step: Valbrand, incensed by raiding renegades and ready for action at last. In the guise of a legendary hero, he would ambush the troublemakers and protect the innocent from harm. Surely, in time he'd be ready to put the mask aside, to reunite with his father, to find and vanquish his enemies—and to claim his rightful place as the most likely successor to the Gullandrian throne.

But the sand trickled downward in the hourglass of time. And Valbrand showed no inclination to give up the mask and emerge from the wilderness. Eric said, "I have kept my vow to you, to remain at your side. I have lied for you. But I refuse to help you tell lies to yourself. The greatest evil awaits you in the south. You must root it out and face it without the Dark Raider's mask."

"When I am ready." Valbrand's tone brooked no further argument.

Eric felt a weariness, a heavy dragging on his soul. "Then I fear that right now there is nothing more to say." He turned for the tunnel.

Valbrand spoke to his back. "I'll stay close tomorrow, in the event of trouble."

"I know it." Eric paused, but he didn't turn.

"You may yet convince her to give up this foolishness."

"It won't happen."

Surely Valbrand had to realize that *he* was the only one who could make Brit go back—by revealing himself to her.

In his mind's eye, Eric saw her—tall, strong, proud...and so very determined.

Then again perhaps it was too late to stop her. Even should Valbrand put aside the mask and show himself to her, she'd still have to try to discover who had sabotaged her plane.

And he'd left her alone for too long. She could wake. If she did, who could say what kind of mischief she'd get up to?

Eric moved into the shadows, never once turning to glance back at his friend. He'd said more than perhaps he should have.

And he knew that Valbrand was already gone.

In her dream Brit rode a fleet black horse. She urged the horse onward, cold wind on her face, her blood pumping in time to the hollow beat of hooves drumming the frozen ground. She saw the sheer cliff before them, the limitless sky beyond. She didn't even try to draw a halt, only urged her dark mount onward, faster and faster toward the yawning chasm ahead.

The horse leaped, hooves churning empty air.

She woke as they fell, twisting, into nothingness.

She lay, covers a tangled mess as usual, on her back. For a dazed moment or two she stared blankly at the cave ceiling above her—arching, uneven, lit by the fickle light of dancing flame shadows.

She turned her head, first to the fire, then to where Eric should have been sleeping.

He wasn't there.

She shot to a sitting position—and saw movement—someone emerging through the tunnel by the underground pool. She was reaching for her pistol when she realized it was only Eric.

She left the pistol on the rock and demanded, "Okay, what's up?"

"Nature calls. I but answer."

She stifled a groan. Leave it to Eric to make a poem of letting her know he'd just stepped out to take a whiz. He approached. She watched him coming, feeling a little curl of warmth down inside. He moved with such sure, easy grace. Dropping his jacket on a rock, he crouched beside her, the action boneless. Fluid.

Her silly heart beat faster. "Looks dark back there. You should have taken a light."

"I know these hills blindfolded—and the tunnels within them."

"How convenient."

"You've made chaos of your bedroll."

"As usual—I was having this incredible dream. I rode a black horse. Over the side of a cliff."

"Were you frightened?"

"Only at the very end. As I fell."

"There are those who believe lessons seek us out in dreams."

"Maybe so. But what a way to go."

"You amaze me."

"Hmm. Amazement. That's good. Right?"

He lifted his hand. It didn't even occur to her to flinch away. The back of his finger traced the line of her jaw, making her flesh warm and tingly, causing those delightful little flares of sensation that faded slowly after his finger had moved on.

She stared into his eyes as his hand moved higher—a light caress against her cheek and then he was smoothing her tangled hair out of her eyes. It took conscious effort not to catch that hand and press her lips to it.

"So brave," he whispered. "And so foolish."

She did flinch away at that. He dropped his hand to his side.

"I gotta wonder," she muttered. "Why is it when a man does what he has to do, that's okay? But when a woman does the same, she's a fool?"

"I didn't call you a fool."

"Close enough."

He frowned. "Is this an argument beginning?"

She lifted her good shoulder in a half-shrug. "Could be."

"Must we continue?"

A moment before, she'd felt all quivery and tender. Now she only felt tired. "You're right. Let's get some sleep."

He rose, went to his own bedroll, dropped down and untied the lace of his left boot. He slanted her a glance as he pulled the boot off. "Will you sit there glaring at me all night, then?"

"Sorry," she mumbled. She pushed the tangle of blankets away from her legs, got up on her knees and set to work straightening out her bed.

They rose before dawn, stoked the fire, fed the horses and ate a cold breakfast of oatcakes, jerky and icy spring water. Together, by the light of the fire, they restacked the blankets and supplies and laid the makings of a fire within a fresh circle of stones. Once they'd prepared the cave for the next time it was needed, they braided the long manes of their horses and tacked up. Through all of it, Eric hardly said a word.

They were ready to head out when, out of nowhere, he announced, "I must speak with you."

Oh, goody. "I was starting to think you never would."

He dropped his horse's reins and sat on a rock near the fire. She holstered her pistol, pulled on her jacket and took a rock next to him.

"Okay," she said. "Spill it."

He stared into the licking flames—clearly in preference to looking at her. "I had hopes you might be convinced to go back before we reached the site where your plane crashed."

"Message received. Loud and clear. You've been telling me I have to go back practically the whole way."

"I wasn't counting on my words alone to make you change your mind. There was also the sight of those men on the trail, the difficult terrain, the storm."

She sighed. ''So much for your hopes.''

He lifted his head and looked at her then. ''I confess, I even had plans to lead you on something of a wild-goose chase.''

She gave him a look. ''I do have a general idea of where we're supposed to be headed, you know. If you led me off in some totally wrong direction—''

He put up a hand, palm out. ''I know. I have finally come to accept that you won't be frightened, overwhelmed or argued from your goal.'' *About time,* she thought. He said, ''So I have reevaluated.''

''Which means?''

''There are things you must know.''

''Such as?''

''I believe as you do. I think your plane was sabotaged.''

She gaped at him for about two seconds. What he'd just admitted was a vindication, of sorts. ''Send up the bottle rockets. We're on the same page at last.'' She started to stand. ''Can we go check it out now?''

''No.''

She sank back to the hard rock. ''Because…?''

''There are guards on it. It isn't safe.''

She asked the pertinent question. ''Guards sent by…?''

He answered grudgingly. ''Your father.''

''And that's a *problem?*''

''They're NIB,'' he said—presumably by way of explanation.

This wasn't adding up. ''NIB? But…then they're on *our* side.''

He looked at her coolly. ''As a whole, the Bureau *is* on 'our side', as you put it.''

"But there are traitors inside it? Is that what you're saying?"

"I don't know that, not beyond a doubt."

"Well, that's reassuring."

"Think. What better way to work against the throne than to infiltrate a governmental organization? All that secret information, right there, at the traitor's fingertips. It's too perfect. We have to assume it has happened."

She looked at him sideways. "This 'we' you mention…it includes my brother, doesn't it?"

For the first time he didn't give her an outright denial. "I am not speaking, at the moment, of your brother."

"No. But I am." She gave it up when he scowled at her. "All right. For now, let's leave my brother out of it." She leaned toward him. "Listen. Really, what's so suspicious here? The guards are NIB, sent at my father's command. They're looking for just what we're looking for—clues as to what made the plane go down."

"They could be doing exactly that."

She waited. He didn't explain himself. She gave up and prodded impatiently, "So? What's your point?"

"The problem is that those men could be working under orders His Majesty never gave them. They could be counteragents—men who have infiltrated the NIB, men who work for your father on one level but on a deeper level are not on his side at all."

She threw up both hands. "How do you know all this?"

"I don't know it, not for certain. But all indications point in that direction."

"What *indications?*"

He only looked at her—an If-I-told-you-that-I'd-have-to-kill-you kind of look.

"That does it." She jumped to her feet. "Let's go. I want to see these guys for myself."

Eric glared up at her. "You are surely the most contrary woman in all this land. Why do you always have to see things for yourself?"

"Indulge me, please. And don't look at me like that." Her request had zero effect. He told her nothing and he went on glaring. She gave up and dropped to the rock again. "I have to say, at this point I just don't know what to believe. For days you've been telling me you're certain my plane going down was an accident. Now you say you think maybe it wasn't—and that there are men guarding it—NIB, but also traitors. You won't tell me how you know this, you just lay it out and expect me to buy it. Why should I? The NIB has been a lot more helpful to me in finding out what I need to know than you've ever been."

His eyes narrowed. "How?"

"Excuse me?"

"How has the NIB been helpful to you?"

"What? That's so surprising? That someone would actually try to *help* me to find out where my brother is?"

"This someone…who is it?"

Brit had had about enough. "You know what? I'm totally, utterly one-hundred percent not getting this."

"I want you to tell me—"

"Uh-uh. Wrong. Not." Now she was the one glaring. She glared and she waited. When he let several seconds elapse without giving any orders, she asked, too sweetly, "Are you listening?"

He nodded.

"Good. Because I have a few points to make and I'd like your undivided attention while make them."

"You have it."

She cleared her throat. "Last night you said I was amazing. Let me return the favor. *You're* amazing. And not in a good way. This is insane. For a while there I thought you and my brother and my father and *your* father were up to something together. Now I don't. Now my take is, you're out of the loop and my father hasn't got a clue. My father and Medwyn indulged what they consider my pointless quest to find my dead brother because it meant I would come here—and hook up with you, thus resulting in wedding bells and the uniting of our families.

"And you and my brother? Well, for some reason that's completely beyond me, you two are just... hanging out up here in the hills. My brother is letting everybody think he's dead while he rides around masked on a black horse playing superhero to the Mystics. I have to say, hel-lo. I don't get it. It makes zero sense to me. If somebody tried to kill me—and I'm guessing they tried to kill Valbrand, too—then there's lots more that's rotten in Denmark than a few renegades. We ought to be working together to deal with the main problem, don't you think? My father and your father should know—not only that my brother's alive, but that there have been nearly successful assassination attempts on his life and on mine."

She paused for a breath—and okay, maybe also because she was hoping he'd speak up and tell her something she didn't already know.

But he kept that fine mouth firmly shut. She looked in his watchful eyes and knew he wasn't going to tell her squat. And for the first time since she woke from her illness and Asta confirmed that her guide had died, she felt hot tears pushing behind her eyes.

Damned if she'd let them fall. ''Oh, Eric. When are you going to get honest with me? When are you going to trust me? When will you tell me what you know so we can finally start working together on this?''

Chapter Thirteen

Eric longed for nothing so much as to open his mouth and tell her that she had it exactly right. What he couldn't say left a bitter taste on his tongue—a bitter taste he would simply have to bear, for he was bound by his vow of silence.

And not only his vow. There was also the hope that had not yet completely run out: that in time Valbrand would come back fully to his true self and willingly reveal himself to the family—and the nation—that thought him dead.

If Eric admitted to Brit now that her brother did live, what would that be but a betrayal of a lifelong friend to whom he'd sworn undying loyalty? And not only that; not just a sacred vow broken; not just the possibility that Valbrand might never forgive him. Were it that alone, at this point, he might have told her anyway.

No. It was what his broken vow might do to Val-brand's fragile equilibrium. He had seen Valbrand living like a creature only half-human. Eric, alone, had lured him from his cave, had coaxed and cajoled until the creature stood upright again and behaved as a man. Eric's vow of silence had been the linchpin that had brought Valbrand home to Gullandria. Eric simply wasn't ready to take the chance of pulling that pin.

Brit was up from her rock again, pacing back and forth before the still-bright fire. She stopped and whirled on him. "Okay, so much for a little give and take. Let me tell you what I intend to do. I'm going—today—to have a look at my plane. And then, once that's done, I'm going back to Isenhalla. I figure I've learned all I can around here."

He knew once she made up her mind to a thing, there was no stopping her. What could he say? *Please don't tell our fathers what you think you know?* Hardly. "You will do what you must."

"You got that much right. Let's go."

"Not yet. Not until you tell me who has *helped* you at the NIB."

She pushed back the sides of her thick jacket and braced her slim hands on her hips, revealing the butt of the weapon she never let get too far from her reach. "Let me get this straight. I get to wander around in the dark—but I'm supposed to tell *you* everything I know."

Eric didn't answer; no words would serve him as well as silence right then. There was no pettiness in her. Given a little time to think it over, she would see that, even in the face of all he hadn't said, it gained her nothing to keep this information from him.

She made a small, grumbling sound. "I keep asking myself, why do I trust you? You won't answer my questions, you won't stop lying to me about my brother...."

"My actions have been trustworthy. Actions should always carry more weight than words."

She plopped to the rock again. "Right. Of course. Thank you for explaining it to me."

"Concerning this person at the NIB..."

"You are relentless."

"The same could, most assuredly, be said of you."

Brit stared into the fire. She *was* going to tell him and she knew it. Putting it off only postponed their getting out of here. "Okay..." She glanced over to meet those waiting eyes. "I have a...what? An ally at the NIB, I guess you could say. Someone I've even started thinking of as a friend."

By then, he was scowling. "This 'ally.' A man?"

"I said a *friend*. It's not a man-woman kind of thing—not that you'd have any business getting heated up about it, if it was."

He didn't argue. But she saw in his eyes that he thought he had every right to object if it turned out there was some other guy on the scene—and, okay, maybe she could understand why he felt that way. Maybe she kind of felt that way herself. He said, "Tell me about this *friend*."

"His name is Jorund Sorenson—Special Agent Jorund Sorenson. I met him about two weeks after I first came here to Gullandria, in July."

"How did this meeting come about?"

"Jorund didn't instigate it, if that's what you're getting at."

"Just tell me how it happened."

"I was nosing around a little, asking questions about Valbrand. And, well, you know how my father is. He got nervous I was going to get myself into some kind of trouble."

"Now, where would His Majesty get an idea like that?"

"Ha-ha. Shall I continue?"

"Please do."

"So...first my dad gets Hauk—my brother-in-law?"

"I know Hauk."

"Well, my dad gets Hauk to put some of his people on me." Hauk Wyborn was the king's warrior. In Gullandria, the king's warrior was the head of an elite fighting squad—a sort of Gullandrian Secret Service, referred to by many as King Osrik's Berserkers—who took their orders directly from the king. "Hauk's men can fight with the best of them. They can also be very discreet. Still, I recognized one of them and had a little talk with my father. Dad promised there'd be no more bodyguards on me. Right. So next, he calls in the NIB—figuring, I suppose, that I wouldn't recognize any of those guys. I didn't. But after four or five days I couldn't help but notice the goons in bad suits tailing me everywhere, looking away whenever I tried to catch their eyes. I got tired of it, so I waylaid one of them. Ducked into a hallway at the National Museum of Norse History and when he came by, looking worried, trying to figure out where I'd gone, I jumped out and shouted, 'Boo!'"

"Charming."

"Believe it or not, I did surprise him. While he was

still sputtering and backing up, I demanded to know who his superior was. He blurted out Jorund's name. I tracked Jorund down at the Bureau offices. At first, you can imagine, he was reluctant to…work with me. But I had a little talk with my father and soon enough I had Special Agent Sorenson checking my rooms at the palace for bugs—even though the bugs were put there at my father's orders. Jorund told me what he knew about Valbrand's disappearance.''

Eric sat up straighter. ''What did he know?''

''Not a lot, really. Only what you said the other morning. That Valbrand went a-Viking and was killed in a storm at sea. Nothing I hadn't already learned. But Jorund would…talk with me about it. You know, we'd take the facts we had and brainstorm with them.''

''Brainstorm…''

''That's when you—''

''Never mind. I'm aware of what the word means. I'm just trying to understand why an NIB special agent would decide to be your 'ally.'''

''You know what? So am I—now. Though you've really told me nothing that proves there are traitors within the NIB.'' Still, Eric had planted the seeds of doubt. It wasn't a good feeling, to find herself wondering at the true loyalties of a man she'd come to trust.

''What else did you learn from this *friend* of yours?''

''We talked about you. Jorund said I'd have trouble getting anything out of you.'' She licked her finger and drew a mark in the air, putting her tongue to the roof of her mouth to make a sizzling sound. "Point for Jorund on that score."

Eric was looking excessively patient. "Did he offer to accompany you here?"

"We talked about it. And we agreed that my showing up with an NIB agent in tow would only make it harder for me to get you to tell me anything."

"Whose reasoning was that?"

"You know, I don't remember."

"Is it possible he simply didn't want to be on that plane with you—or anywhere nearby when you met your tragic end?"

Defensiveness curled through her, tightening her stomach, making her edgy and fed up with talking. "Anything's possible—can we go now?"

Those watchful eyes were on her. She thought for sure he would have more to say. But in the end, he only stood. "As you wish. Let me douse the fire."

They emerged from the cave to find the dawn coming, the sun not yet risen, a soft glow on the far horizon. The thin layer of snow from yesterday's storm crunched beneath the horses' hooves as they picked their way upward to the crest of the hill and then down the other side.

The new day was starting out warmer even than the day before. As the sun rose, the snow melted. Within a few brief hours it lay in shrinking patches here and there on the trail. They reached the rim of Drakveden Fjord at a little past ten and paused, still mounted, to admire the view. It was a sheer drop-off, walls of rough black rock going down and down through layers of mist. Far below, faintly, Brit could see a thick ribbon of water, gleaming. Across the yawning misty space, a waterfall tumbled from the facing cliffs, white and foaming, roaring as it fell.

Brit checked her compass. They'd been traveling parallel with the fjord for several miles, but this was the first time the trail had met up with it. She spoke to Eric, raising her voice to compete with the roar of the falls. "Where do we go down?"

"We follow the rim for another two kilometers. Then the trail begins a slow descent."

"We're close."

He nodded, turning his horse to the trail once more.

Soon they reached the place where the trail began going down. They followed the twists and turns, ducking hanging tree branches, until they reached a spot about midway along. For another hour they moved due west, climbing awhile, then moving down, then up again, most of the time with the waters of the fjord in sight below them.

Finally, when they'd been climbing for some time, Eric turned his horse from the trail, away from the water. They wove their way through the trees for several yards and came to a small clearing.

He dismounted, taking his rifle from the saddle holster and binoculars from his saddlebag. "Hobble your horse. We go down now, to the crash site. The trail is narrow from here on, little more than a rocky ledge. It's safer—and quieter—to go on foot."

She thought of the roving bands of renegades, of the bears and Gullandrian mountain cats that she knew roamed the hills. "You think it's safe to leave the horses here alone?"

"Safer than to try to ride them any closer to the

crash site. We'll be quieter on foot." He must have read her look. "Yes, they could be gone—stolen, or attacked by predators—when we return, if that's what you're wondering."

She swallowed. "Yeah, that was what I was wondering."

"We have to take that chance—unless, that is, you'd prefer to turn around?"

"Nice try." She dismounted. "Let's go."

They went back the way they'd come, rejoining the trail at about the same spot they'd left it and forging on to the west. In half a mile or so, they came out onto a point with a clear view of the gorge floor and the fjord below.

"Stay low." Eric dropped to a crouch and signaled her to follow. They crept to the edge, where two waist-high boulders blocked the view as they ducked behind them.

"What now?"

"First, look between the space in the rocks. Down there. Do you see?"

She saw the narrow spit of land where she'd brought down the Skyhawk, saw the crumpled fuselage not far from the trees at the end of the rocky ground. "My plane," she said, "or what's left of it." A moment of silence elapsed and then she asked, "What else?"

"We wait," he said.

"For...?"

He set his rifle carefully aside and indicated the binoculars he'd taken from his saddlebag. Then he pointed to a wide gray-bellied white cloud drifting near the sun. "That cloud will soon cover the sun and minimize the chance that sunlight will reflect off the lenses and give our position away to anyone below.''

"Waiting. Great. Not my favorite activity.''

He grunted. "I have noticed.''

Time crawled by. About five endless minutes later, the sun slipped behind the outer edge of the cloud. Eric brought up the binoculars and peered with them through a gap in the rocks. He scanned the terrain below. "There,'' he whispered, more to himself than to her. "And there…'' He gave her the binoculars. "Look for yourself. There are three of them visible from this vantage point.'' He guided the binoculars to her face. "First look straight across, to the opposite slope, then down a little…''

She picked out an armed man, in the trees on the hillside opposite, but below the point where they crouched. "I see him.''

"Lower now. Track west—to your left.''

She found him. "Okay. That's two.''

And the third…he's difficult to make out, near the base of this trail, after it flattens out, still in the trees, a short distance before they give way to bare ground.'' He took hold of the binoculars again, just enough to lower them to the right place. "There? You see him?''

She focused. Found the man. He was dressed like the others, in camo fatigues, dark boots and a plain black watch cap, a rifle in his hands. His broad back was to her—at first. But then, for a moment, he turned his head. She got a look, at his face, a three-quarter view. It was a fleshy, roundish face, with a blunt jaw, a small mouth and close-set eyes…

She lowered the binoculars. "I know him. I mean, I've seen him before.''

"Where?"

"That first day I went to the Bureau offices. He was coming out of Jorund's office as I was going in."

"So...a subordinate of your supposed friend?"

"It's as good a guess as any—and I don't like the way you say *supposed*."

"But you are willing now to admit those men are NIB?"

"Since I know one of them and I saw him at the Bureau offices—sure. It's not a big leap. But you know what? It's pure paranoia to think that means they're automatically traitors."

"They've been guarding this area for days now. And there is a fourth man, somewhere nearby, probably on the hillside below us, not visible from here. And not only those four—there are two more, at the boat they used to get here. They rotate in guarding the plane. We can't be certain when they'll change shifts—or if, right now, there are five of them nearby, or even all six."

"How do you know all this?"

His response to that was another of those oh-so-patient looks. He said, "The plane is unsalvageable. Your father believes you had an accident, that's all. Word has been sent that you survived the crash and a renegade's attack and are safe at my family's village. Those men have had plenty of time to look things over and remove any equipment His Majesty might have wanted saved. They should have been gone days ago. Yet they remain. Why else would they stay except in hopes that you might return—as you are doing—and give them another chance to finish what they started?"

"Eric, you don't know what my father thinks. You

have minimal communication with him. You send him radio messages, right, telling him your version of what's up? And he replies in kind."

"That is correct."

"Maybe he suspects what you and I suspect. That somebody helped my plane to go down. Maybe he has those men guarding it so that, if any of the real assassins show up to look over their handiwork, those men can deal with them."

"Your reasoning is faulty."

"Gee, thanks. Why?"

"You know His Majesty. If he believed you'd survived an assassination attempt, he'd have ordered you back to Isenhalla. He'd want you near him, where he could make certain you were safe. And he'd want to interview you in depth to learn everything you know in order to find and punish the ones who dared to do such a thing."

His argument made sense. Too much sense. "I'm still not going to just *assume* that those men are traitors. I'm not going to—"

Eric cut her off by muttering grimly, "Enough. You've seen them. We can't risk hailing them and we can't be sure how many more of them are out there than the three we can find. We will return now to my aunt's village."

"The hell we will."

He was glaring again. "What more can we do?"

"We've got to find out if they're really my father's men—or not."

"There is no way to find out for certain without the chance of—"

She cut *him* off that time. "I have a plan."

His lip curled in distaste. "I don't like it."

"You haven't even heard it yet."

"I know by the look in your eye that I'm not going to like it."

"Just listen. Just let me explain."

"Do I have a choice?"

"Not about this. Oh, Eric. We have all these suspicions—suspicions that mean nothing without some kind of proof."

"I see it in your eyes. To get your proof could mean your death."

"Not if we're careful—and we might just find out those guys down there are on our side, after all."

"No. It's too dangerous." He dropped the binoculars and took her by the arms. "Listen. Let me take you back. I'll gather some men. We'll return here. We'll capture the agents below and question them. We'll discover—"

"Zilch." She pulled free. "They'll just tell you that they're NIB sent to guard the plane."

His square jaw was set. "If they're traitors, we'll find out."

"By torture? No, thanks. My way's a lot more direct and my way no one has to get hurt."

"I don't like it," he said for the third time.

"You haven't even heard me out yet. Please. Just listen for a minute." He looked at her as if he wanted to strangle her—but he kept his mouth shut. It was her chance. She took it. "We'll go down there now—carefully, making sure the guys on the opposite slope don't spot us, watching for any others as we go. We'll circle the one I recognize—yes, we'll have to be careful, not give him any chance to signal the others. You go behind him, get up close. I'll step out and say hello.''

He blinked. ''Hello. You'll say...hello.''

''That's right. If he was sent here to kill me, he'll probably try it. Then we'll both get a chance to stop him.'' She said the rest, though she hated to have to say it. ''And we'll know if my friend at the NIB wasn't really any kind of friend at all.''

He stared at her as if she'd suddenly sprouted horns and a tail. ''This is madness.''

''Not madness. Dangerous, possibly. But we're going to make it work. And no one is going to get hurt.''

He made a growling sound. ''You delude yourself. You could be killed. If the three Norns of destiny smile on us, you might survive. But in any case, if that fellow down there points his rifle at you, he will die. I will see to it.''

''No. Now, that isn't the plan.''

''He will die.''

''Eric. You're not listening.''

''Because you are talking dangerous nonsense.''

She decided to let that insulting remark pass and stick to the point. ''I don't want anyone to get hurt. I mean it. There's been enough bloodshed around here lately, thank you very much. If he points his gun at me, you can jump him. We'll shoot to wound if we have to—but the idea is to get through this without a shot being fired. Shots will only bring the others down on us.''

''It's madness.''

''You keep saying that.''

''I won't be a part of it.''

''Oh, no? Then what.''

"I am going back to the village. Now. You are coming with me."

"No. I'm not. Go back by yourself if you think you have to, but—"

He put up a hand. There was silence. Somewhere in the trees behind them, a bird warbled out a brief, bright song. At last he spoke. "What, by all the frozen towers of Hel, is a man to do with you?"

"Eric."

He didn't really answer, just made a low, furious sound and muttered what must have been a truly bad Gullandrian oath, though he spoke too low for her to make out the words.

"It's the only way," she said.

"It's not—and I have it. You'll stay here. I'll go down and—"

"No. It has to be me he sees. He might or might not attack you for any number of reasons. But if he tries to shoot me, well, the only reason he'd do that is because he—and most likely Jorund Sorenson—is part of the plot to get rid of me."

Something happened in his eyes.

"Don't," she said.

He was utterly still.

"I mean it, Eric. If you try to…stop me now, if you do something to physically restrain me from going down there, you will only be putting off the inevitable. I'm going to go. And if you mess with me now, I'll just end up doing it alone as soon as I can escape you."

The look on his face at that moment was frightening. And then, in a movement so tiny she barely saw it even though she was looking straight at him, he shook his head. Or maybe not shook it, exactly. Just gave it a sharp, minute jerk to the left. It might have been a twitch—except that Eric Greyfell was not a man prone to twitching.

She didn't dare turn from him, didn't trust him not to try to knock her out, or jump her for her own good. But she was absolutely certain that there was someone behind her, and that Eric had just signaled that someone—in the negative.

Like a bright light exploding on in darkness, she got it. "Valbrand?" she asked Eric quietly. He only went on looking at her, barely controlled fury in his eyes. So she spoke, still not turning, to the presence behind her. "Valbrand. It's you, isn't it?"

Chapter Fourteen

No one answered—until Eric said, "You're mistaken. There's no one there."

It was true, of course. There was no longer anyone behind her. She had a clear sense that whoever it was had melted back into the trees. She turned and saw exactly what she expected to see: nothing but bare ground and, a little farther on, tall, thick evergreens. She turned to Eric again. "So then," she said cheerfully, "we do have backup—the, uh, Dark Raider would be my guess."

"I said there is no one." He was really, really mad.

She strove to keep it light. "Well, yes. You did. But just because you said it doesn't make it true."

He hooked the binoculars to his belt beneath his jacket and reached for his rifle. "If you're determined to do this, let's go." He remained utterly furious. It occurred to her that she'd never seen him so enraged. And all at once, she had the hollow, awful feeling that he would never forgive her for forcing him to do this.

Heartsickness, all the more powerful for being totally unanticipated, washed over her in a heavy, dragging wave. Without thinking, she grabbed his arm. "Do you have to be so angry?"

He froze. His hand was on the rifle. She clutched his coat and the hard forearm beneath it. He looked down at her grasping fingers as if they repulsed him. Then he said, very quietly, "As much as I crave your touch, now is not the time."

She knew he was right. She shouldn't have touched him. She let go. He looked in her face then, his eyes green ice. She stared into those eyes and discovered something about herself she would have preferred not to know.

She wanted—*yearned*—to give in to him. To let him lead her away from the precipice, back to the safety of his aunt's friendly village. To say what women have said since the beginning of time: *Yes, all right. You're bigger and stronger and you want to take care of me. We'll do it your way....*

She yearned to.

But she couldn't. It wasn't in her to follow—not when she was certain that she was in the right. Yes, it was dangerous. But not to take the chance would leave them with their suspicions and their theories and not much else. This way, they might inch a fraction closer to discovering who their real enemies were.

"Can't you see, Eric? We have to do this."

He gave her no answer. His face remained closed against her. He would only say, again, "Let's go."

* * *

Eric on point, Brit right behind him, they made their way down slowly, watching where they put their feet, catching branches before they ran into them, pushing them aside, releasing them gently, exercising constant vigilance to make as little sound as possible. Careless footfalls could dislodge rocks and pebbles that would tumble to the gorge below, gathering momentum, collecting other bits of debris as they went and signaling their presence to the men with the guns.

The trail was narrow—hardly more than a sliver of ledge in places—cut raggedly into the rocky side of the hill. Luckily for them, rather than the bare black rock that rimmed so much of the fjord, here, the trees grew close all around, providing cover from seeking eyes.

The farther they got without incident, the more certain Brit became that something very bad was going to happen any second now. Her whole body felt prickly, the skin tight and twitchy at the back of her neck. She was wet beneath the arms—and it wasn't all that warm out. No, this was the sweat of pure animal fear. She knew it was coming—from behind or above: someone would jump on her or shoot her or throw a knife, *thwack,* right between her shoulderblades.

Still they kept moving. Nobody attacked them.

She tried not to obsess on that other guy, the fourth guard they'd never spotted, the one Eric had said had to be around there somewhere. Really, where else would be as logical as lurking close to the trail?

But the miracle happened: nothing. They kept moving downward. They were almost to the bottom, perhaps fifty yards from where the ground flattened out. Very soon now they'd be closing in on that cohort of Jorund's—that is, if he was anywhere near where he'd been when they pinpointed his location from above.

She heard rustling—ten or twelve yards up and behind her. She stopped, stood absolutely still. So did Eric. They waited—straining to see. But the trees were too thick.

And then—in a few seconds that only seemed like a lifetime—the rustling stopped.

They waited some more. Brit wondered if the Dark Raider had just taken on that mysterious fourth guard—or if it was only some unwary creature, scrabbling along the hillside.

They went on, stopping dead again when Brit stepped on a rock wrong and it went sliding off down the hill. But fortune smiled on them. The rock caught in an exposed tree root before it really got rolling.

Silence. They went on.

At last they reached the floor of the gorge. There were maybe twenty yards of forest ahead of them. And then the open rocky ground, her plane and, farther on, the jewel-blue fjord waters.

Now, to find Jorund's associate before the associate found them. Eric gestured for her to follow. They left the trail and moved into the trees, creeping along, every slight crunch at each footfall sounding loud as cannon fire.

Eric stopped, ducked, signaled her down. She crouched beside him. He pointed.

She picked out the combat boots and the fatigues tucked into them—maybe twenty feet from them, facing away. Way close. Way scary. Her heart pounded in her ears. The boots began to move, turning with agonizing slowness, as if the man who wore them had heard something and was cautiously seeking the source of the sound.

Brit held her breath—realized she was doing it—let it out with slow care. The boots had stopped, blunt toes facing their direction, as if the agent knew they were lurking there.

Thank God for Eric ordering her down—crouched as they were, the man must be looking right over their heads. The boots began to move again. In a few seconds she and Eric stared once more at the heels.

Eric touched her, the slightest brush of his hand against her good shoulder, to get her attention. She looked at him and he gestured, a circular movement, tracing in the air the path he would take through the trees to get around to the other side of the owner of the heavy boots.

It seemed such a long, long way to go soundlessly. The crack of a broken branch or a foot placed wrong, and the man who wore the boots might spot him, open fire....

Eric could die doing this.

The simple sentence ricocheted its way around her brain.

She had known it before, of course she had. As she had known that she herself might die.

But right now, it was...too real, too imminent. It was the sweat beneath her arms, the shiver down her back, the too-loud, too-fast, hurtful beating of her heart....

Eric could die.

And how would she bear it?

He looked at her. And she looked back at him.

She knew that he knew how close she was...to shaking her head. To mouthing, *No. Let's not do this, after all. Let's just go back.*

But somehow she didn't shake her head. She didn't mouth anything. She only looked into his eyes until the moment passed.

And then, very deliberately, she nodded.

He began to creep away from her. It was incredible, how quietly he could move. He wove his way through the trees, his steps without sound. She alternately watched him...and the boots. The boots did move, this way and that. The movements of a man on guard with no perceived danger nearby.

Too soon, she couldn't see Eric anymore.

She crouched there, watching the boots, her pulse a tattoo in her ears, reminding herself now and then to breathe, slowly realizing she had no clue when she ought to make her move.

Was Eric in position yet—was there even a position for him to *get* into? A tree big enough to hide behind, a crouch low enough that the man in the heavy boots wouldn't look down and see him?

Silently she railed at herself. It was a bad plan. An exceedingly stupid plan. It was so bad and so stupid it was no plan at all. Eric would die and she would either die right after him—or wish she had.

Oh, why hadn't she listened to him? Why had she insisted her way was the only way?

She swallowed. And then, carefully, silently, she reached under her jacket and wrapped her fingers around the grip of her SIG.

No. She let it go, smoothed her jacket down to cover

it. Its weight might feel reassuring in her hand, but she couldn't be carrying it in plain sight when she hailed the agent. He mustn't feel threatened. And if he saw the gun, how else would he feel? He might shoot her just because he thought she was planning to shoot him.

And then what would they learn from executing this bad, stupid plan of hers?

She strained all her senses, listening.

Nothing but a slight wind whispering in the trees, a bird calling far off. The boots faced the other way— not moving.

Were those boots…too still?

She thought, *He's seen something, in the trees. Let it not be Eric.*

And surely Eric must be in position—whatever that meant—by now.

And the boots…the boots were starting to move, cautiously, away.

It was the moment to act. She knew it. She didn't know exactly *how* she knew. But this was no time to question her instincts.

Right now her instincts were just about all she had.

As quietly as she could, she crept forward, bent at the waist, but up on her feet. Each step took an eternity, yet somehow, between one breath and the next, she was there. Close enough that three more steps would bring her to where she could reach out and touch the man with the rifle, in the combat boots and the camo fatigues. He had his back to her, his rifle ready in his hands. He had heard something. He peered into the trees.

Time to do it.

She stood to her height and boldly stepped forward. "Ahem."

The agent went still—and then he turned. He saw her, standing no more than six feet from him. The close-set eyes widened. The small mouth formed an O. Under less scary circumstances, his expression might have brought a chuckle.

Now, though, she didn't feel like laughing at all. She had to force a wide grin. "Hey. Am I ever glad to see you."

The agent blinked. "Your Highness?"

"You bet."

The agent raised his rifle.

So much for my *ally* at the NIB, she thought. And then everything happened at once, in that strangely slow way that things tend to happen when you have to act and act fast—or die.

She ducked—well, that was the bad, stupid plan, wasn't it? And Eric rose soundlessly from behind the agent, seeming to materialize out of thin air with the butt of his rifle held high in both strong hands. He slammed the rifle butt into the back of the agent's head before the agent could readjust his aim and fire down at her.

There was the awful thick sound of the something hard connecting with the agent's skull. And the man dropped like a safe, without managing to get off a shot. His rifle fell with him, unfired, to the forest floor.

Slowly she straightened and stared down at the slack face below her. There—his chest moved. Yes! Still alive. Her bad, stupid plan had worked perfectly. They knew what they needed to know and everyone was still breathing.

She didn't get all that much time to pat herself on the back, though. It appeared that things weren't so perfect, after all. Eric had dropped to a crouch, set his rifle aside and whipped something thin and black from his boot. *Snick.* A gleaming blade shot from the black handle.

Sheesh. Hauk had a knife like that. She hadn't had a clue that Eric had one, too.

Brit stared down, not quite believing what she was seeing as Eric hooked the unconscious man beneath the chin, yanking his head farther back, knocking his watch cap off in the process—and exposing a too-vulnerable expanse of bare neck.

"No!" Brit whispered the word with such force it echoed in her ears like a shout. She went to her haunches and grabbed Eric's knife arm before he could slit the unconscious agent's throat. "Nobody dies."

Eric's eyes glittered with a feral light. "That's the second time you've grabbed me when you had no business doing it."

She didn't let go this time. She couldn't. "Eric. I beg you. Don't kill him."

His lip curled, wolflike. "*He* would have killed *you*."

"But he didn't. Eric. *Please.*"

For a terrible moment she was certain there was no way she could stop him. He would shake her off and slit the unconscious man's throat.

But then, with a low grunt of pure disgust, he flicked the blade back into the knife handle and let go of the man's chin. There was blood, on his pants, at the knee, where the agent's head had pressed against him. She wondered if the fellow would survive in any case.

The knife disappeared in Eric's boot. He grabbed his waiting rifle, then took the agent's pistol from its shoulder holster, dropped out the clip and threw it into the trees. He tossed the pistol in the opposite direction. Then he picked up the man's rifle and shoved it at Brit. She took it.

"We dare not linger," he muttered. His fury was palpable, like the beating of hot wings on the chill air. "The others will be on us." He turned without another word and headed for the trail.

She put the safety on the rifle and followed.

The unconscious man groaned. He was waking at last from his abrupt, unwelcome sleep.

Valbrand, safe behind the mask, crouched a few feet from the man's boots. He had two lengths of cord and a gag at his side and the traitor's own pistol, loaded again and pointed at the traitor's heart, in his hand. It had been approximately fifteen minutes since his bold and cheeky little sister and his angry bloodbound friend had strode off toward the trail. By now they should be almost at their waiting horses. And safe.

Yes, there was another agent, up higher on the trail. But he would present no challenge to them. Valbrand had considered killing him, but in the end had left him alive, unarmed, gagged and tied to a tree, for his colleagues to find—if something with sharp teeth and claws didn't get to him first. If he lived, that traitor would have an interesting story to tell.

Behind the mask Valbrand smiled. He knew his smile, once thought the most charming in all of the land, was hideous now. He could feel the ugliness of it, ruined flesh pulling in the most bizarre ways. That was the wonder of the mask. The ugliness hidden behind smooth black leather.

Would the bound agent on the hillside dare to tell his comrades that the Dark Raider had attacked him? Would they think he'd gone mad if he did?

Valbrand had an intimate knowledge of madness. For a long while, until Eric had found him and begun the endless, unhappy process of luring him back to the bleak world of sanity, he'd found a certain wild comfort in madness.

But then, being mad was not the same as merely having others believe you to be. More frustrating, most likely. Less…consuming.

And, since Valbrand had decided to let the man before him live as well, this one and the agent on the hill could corroborate each other's stories. That made them at least a fraction more likely to be believed. Less likely to be thought out of their mutual minds.

And that was good.

Let them all believe and let them fear and wonder….

Let whoever lurked—a puppet master pulling lethal strings—behind these recent deadly games, beware.

The time *was* coming. Valbrand knew it and hated that he knew it. And yes, Eric had it right: Valbrand dreaded facing his father and his people. It *would* be a thousand times more difficult than the bleak horror of what had gone before.

But he would do it. Somehow. When the time was right.

For now, though, there was the consoling feel of the

mask against his ruined face. And this traitor, groaning at his feet.

The traitor opened his eyes. They widened. Good.

Valbrand rose to his height, pistol trained on the stunned face below him. "Your name, traitor."

The man groaned.

Valbrand cocked the pistol. It wasn't necessary to cock it, not with a gun like this one. But cocking it did make such a satisfying sound. "Your name."

The man lifted his head. "Agent...Hans Borger."

"And whom do you serve, Hans Borger?"

Borger groaned again and let his head drop. "My king."

"You lie. I should kill you now." Valbrand gestured with the gun. "Over. To your belly, dog, where you belong."

With another groan, the agent started to roll, sliding one hand down as he did it. Valbrand chuckled and held up the contact device in his left hand. "Looking for this?" The dog's eyes widened—then narrowed in defeat. Valbrand dropped the device to the ground and crushed it under his boot. "Now roll."

Hans Borger obeyed. Swiftly, aware of the danger of temporarily setting the weapon aside, Valbrand took the waiting lengths of cord and bound the agent hand and foot. He tied the gag last, tightly.

Then he picked up the gun and rose again to his feet. "When they find you, tell them that Princess Brit and Prince Eric Greyfell disarmed you with ease. They spared your worthless life, as do I, the Dark Raider. This game that you and your cohorts may have thought almost over has only now begun. It will end in shameful defeat and slow, painful death for all who dared to dream they could bring down the House of Thor.''

The dog on the ground grunted behind his gag and struggled fitfully against the cords that bound him. There was blood matting his close-cut pale hair.

Valbrand holstered his weapon. "Would that I had more time. We could speak…in depth. I would show you the many ways I know to make a sharp knife sing. But I fear the dogs you run with will come looking for you soon. So I shall leave you now, to the mercy of the traitors who own you. May they punish you cruelly for your failure, after they laugh in your face when you tell them that the princess you were sent to kill outsmarted you and that you let Eric Greyfell come up behind you without your knowing, armed only with the wrong end of a rifle." He paused, considered, then advised, "Perhaps you shouldn't even mention your conversation with me. So many believe I am only a myth, a story told to children, by firelight, on long winter nights. So if you were to tell them that you spoke with me…hmm. Were I your superior, I might begin to think you mad.''

Agent Borger had little constructive to contribute in reply. A gag will do that. He grunted and struggled, a pitiful sight.

Valbrand had said all that needed saying. Grinning behind the mask, he turned and vanished into the trees.

Chapter Fifteen

Eric, grim-faced and speaking to Brit only when absolutely necessary, kept them on the move for the remainder of the day. They crossed paths with no dangerous animals—on two legs or four. And they made good time.

Still, the long fingers of twilight had slipped down the slopes of the hills when they rode their tired horses out of the trees and onto the hard-packed dirt street of Asta's village. Light glowed, warm and welcoming, from the high-set narrow windows of the longhouses, and Sigrid's oldest boy, Brokk, named after his father, came running out to meet them.

"Grandmother Asta asked me to wait for you." The redheaded, freckle-faced boy, all of eleven, smiled in pride at being granted such a great responsibility. The boy said Asta was tending one of the village women.

"She makes a new baby tonight." The boy beamed. "I've left the fire well tended. And I'm good with the horses. Will you allow me to see to your mounts?"

For the first time since their argument at the lookout point above the wreckage of the plane, Eric smiled. "We would be pleased and grateful to leave our horses in your capable hands."

They dismounted and the boy took both sets of reins.

Eric turned to her, his smile a memory. He spoke curtly. "Take the traitor's rifle and whatever you need from the saddlebags."

She did as he told her, feeling exhausted and heartsick—and aching for the sight of Asta's kind, wrinkled face. It looked like a long, grim night ahead, with Asta gone to another longhouse and Brit alone with Mr. Cheerful.

Brokk said, "There's shepherd's pie waiting in the warming oven. I will see to the horses, then tell Grandmother that you've returned safely. She'll be glad of the news." The boy headed for the horse barn behind Asta's longhouse, leaving the two of them standing in the street.

After a moment, not even sparing her a glance, Eric turned for the house. Reluctantly Brit trailed after, feeling like a very bad child and resenting it—a lot.

Inside, Brit went straight to her sleeping bench and dropped her things on her bed furs. She still had the rifle.

"Give it here," Eric grumbled.

She handed it over, and he put it, along with his own rifle and the shotgun, in the rack above the door.

She took off her coat, hung it on a peg and then went to put her things away.

They shared a truly toxic silence as they washed their hands and faces and got out the pie, set a simple table and sat down to eat. She stolidly chewed and swallowed and avoided Eric's eyes—which wasn't difficult. He didn't show any eagerness to look at her, either.

It was really bad. She wished she could do something, say something, to try to get him to...

What?

Forgive her for being right about her admittedly wild plan that had given them the first piece of solid information as to who might be behind the plot to kill her?

And maybe, while he was forgiving her, he could stop being mad at her because she stepped in before he could slit a man's throat?

The problem was, the longer he scowled and growled, the more she started thinking that she was getting pretty mad herself. Okay, she was an action junkie. She didn't like to sit around, considering all the angles, when something could be *done*.

Her plan had been far from well thought out. But damn it, it had worked, hadn't it?

She sent him an angry glance. He glared back at her.

They ate the rest of the food, cleared off and washed the heavy plates. By then she was certain that if she stayed cooped up with him much longer, there would be yelling and throwing of plates.

"I'm going over to bathhouse," she announced into

the awful, furious silence. "I'll be back in an hour or so."

"I'll go with you."

"No. I'll go alone. I don't need you to—"

"I'd like a bath myself." He said it flatly. The look in his eyes said he'd also like to grab her and shake her till she pleaded for mercy and never again dared to have a plan of her own.

"Fine. Whatever. It's a free country—more or less."

They gathered what they needed and went out into the night.

In the bathhouse, Brit took off her clothes and her bandage and indulged in a shamefully long, hot shower. Her wound was healed enough by then that she could handle bandaging it herself. And she did, with gauze and tape, before she put on clean clothes, her lightest long underwear first. The underwear was made of silk, but it was still your basic long johns design, a long-sleeved T-shirt and super-lightweight knit bottoms. Over the long johns, she pulled on a sweater and jeans. Bedtime was coming, so she dispensed with a bra.

She emerged into the night again, hoping she had taken long enough that Eric would have already gone back. The short walk to the longhouse would have been much more pleasant without him scowling at her side.

But no. There he was, waiting, his face a bleak mask. He saw her and he turned without a word and headed up the street.

Oh, boy, wasn't this fun? She hung back, walking

slowly, hoping he would charge on ahead and leave her, for a few precious moments anyway, alone.

He didn't. When he realized she wasn't hustling to catch up with him, he stopped and glared back at her. "Are you coming?" In spite of the question mark at the end, it was an impatient command.

She pressed her lips together—hard—to keep something loud and shrill from getting out. And then she picked up her pace.

Back in the longhouse, it was more of the same. Silence and total avoidance of anything resembling eye contact.

The night might be young, but it showed no likelihood of turning the least bit enjoyable. And the day had been long. And tomorrow, she was going to have to figure out how she'd get out of the Vildelund and back to Isenhalla. Maybe Eric would contact her father and have him send some small aircraft to pick her up.

Or maybe she'd have to head for the Black Mountains. The high, snow-capped range about twenty miles due south of the village stood between the Vildelund and the more civilized world on the other side.

Whatever. One way or another, she was out of here tomorrow. Jorund had to be dealt with. And she wanted to have a long heart-to-heart with her father. It was about time somebody told the king what the hell was going on.

She brushed her teeth and went to her sleeping bench, took off the top layer of clothes and climbed beneath the furs wearing her socks and her long johns. With so much hostility thickening the air, it took a while to get to sleep.

But she was tired. Her bed might be hard, but she'd grown used to it by then. And the furs felt so soft and comforting around her....

Eric waited until he was certain she slept. Then he pulled on his coat and grabbed his boots and slipped out the door, pausing at the stoop to put the boots on.

In the trees behind the horse paddock, Valbrand waited, a darker shadow among shadows. His rare black Gullandrian gelding was hobbled a few feet away, nosing and nibbling the cold ground.

"The traitor?" Eric asked.

"He lives. I left him bound and gagged and awaiting the tender mercies of the others."

"The one higher on the hillside?"

"I did the same for him."

"Did you get anything from either of them?"

"There was no opportunity to ask questions of the one up on the hill. I took his rifle and his pistol."

"And the other?"

"His name. Agent Hans Borger. I regret there was no time to learn more."

"At least we know now that our suspicions concerning the infiltration of the NIB have merit."

"Thanks to the clever actions of my irrepressible little sister."

Eric heard the rare smile in Valbrand's voice and didn't like it—not now, not on this subject. "Can't you see that the woman rushes headlong toward her own death at every opportunity? She is suicidal in her heedlessness."

"She looked quite healthy to me when you led her away."

"Yes, she came away unharmed. This time." Eric

stuck his fists in the pockets of his coat. "She leaves tomorrow for the south."

"Your choice—or hers?"

"She has said she will go. It is probably, at this point, the only issue on which we agree."

"What of your marriage?"

"What of it? She refuses me at every turn."

"Perhaps you give her reason to refuse you?"

An angry rejoinder rose in his throat. He swallowed it. "I only want to keep her safe."

"Even I can see she's not a woman who seeks safety. Perhaps if you wish finally to claim her, you will have to take her as she is."

Eric glared straight-on into the dark eyes behind the mask. "Do you lecture me now, my friend?"

"I but offer…an objective view."

An objective view. Now, there was an irony. Valbrand was supposed to be the leader. Providing an objective view had always been Eric's responsibility. He grumbled, "I am in no mood to take what you offer with any grace."

"As you wish." The black horse tossed his fine head and snorted. Valbrand spoke to the animal softly, "Easy, Starkavin. All is well." Then he turned to Eric again. "By what route will she return to the palace?"

"We've yet to speak of that."

"Whichever way she goes, there will be danger."

"Must you remind me?"

"When danger is inevitable—why not make use of it?"

An owl hooted, somewhere in the dark. Overhead, beyond the trees, the quarter moon dangled from a star. The night was cloudless and very still.

Eric asked, "What are you getting at?"

Valbrand moved closer and pitched his voice to a whisper. "Why not guide our enemies to waylay us on our terms?"

Brit was sitting at the table in her long johns and heavy socks, one of Asta's knitted shawls thrown across her shoulders, when Eric came sneaking through the door, his boots in his hands.

She had a pretty good idea where he'd been: out to meet Valbrand. But she wasn't going to challenge him about it. She was a little sick of challenges at the moment, thank you.

He said, "What are doing out of bed?" The question was pure challenge. Of course.

What business is it of yours? she thought. She stared at the lamp she'd lighted. It sat on the table before her, giving off a warm golden glow that didn't comfort her in the least. "I woke up. I was alone. For the first time since late this morning, there was no one here to glare or bark at me." She looked at Eric. "I found it kind of…pleasant. I decided to get up and enjoy the peace and quiet." Sadly, she hadn't enjoyed the absence of hostility as much as she'd hoped to. She'd started thinking about Jorund and what a complete idiot she'd been on that score. Yeah—duh. Sure, an NIB special agent had just been longing to be her *friend*….

Eric shrugged. He turned to hang his jacket on a peg and set his boots beside the door. When he faced her again, it was only to say, "I bid you good-night, then."

It came to her on a wave of frustrated misery that this was impossible. It really had to stop. "Eric…"

He paused a few feet from her—on his way to his sleeping bench. "What is it now?"

Her irritation spiked again. Oh, why even bother to try to get through to him?

Because I care for him—a whole lot—and I can't stand to leave it like this.

She gathered the warm shawl a little closer around her, seeking a comfort she didn't find. "Look. Can we just get past this? I'm leaving tomorrow. We've been...friends, haven't we? Friends shouldn't part in anger."

His gray-green gaze swept over her, burning where it touched. "We are much more than friends. And you know it. Why will you constantly insist on belittling the bond between us?"

She wanted to shout at him—and she held it back; to reach out to him—but he wouldn't like it.

Stifled at every turn, she couldn't sit still. She stood from the end of the bench. He backed up a step, as if he thought she might dare to put her hands on him.

And really, the voice of fairness whispered in her ear, why wouldn't he think it? She'd grabbed him twice today, both times when the last thing he wanted was her touching him.

She bit her lip and went to the stove. Behind the window in the stove door, she could see the red flames licking. She stared into them, gathering calm about her like the shawl around her shoulders, thinking that this was for sure a first: Brit Thorson, striving for calm and reason.

Wouldn't Liv and Elli have a great big fat laugh? And her mother? Ingrid would never believe it.

She turned to him again and spoke slowly, choosing

each word with care. "I don't belittle what's between us. I swear I don't. I do think of you as a friend and I think it's important—to be friends with a man who...I care for so much."

His face remained set against her, but his gaze ran over her, furious—and hungry. She knew he wanted to shout rude things at her. And that he also wanted to do things—sexual things—the kind of things a man like Eric would never do to someone who was only a *friend.*

And she? All right, yes. She wanted him to do those things. With all of her yearning body.

And every beat of her aching heart.

But first there was what had to be said. She pleaded, "Look. Just say it, will you? Whatever you want to say to me, just do it, just get it out."

"You are serious?"

"As a bullet through the heart."

"You won't like it."

"I don't expect to like it. I just think it's what you have to say...and what I've got to stand here and take."

It must have made sense to him. He laid it on her, his voice low and deep, his tone as intense as the hunger in his eyes. "I fear for you—fear you see this trouble before us as some kind of tempting, risky game. I begin to think that there is but one thing that you do with slow care, and that is eat those bright candies you love. I close my eyes—and I see you dead, your pretty neck slit for some chance you just had to take. You are...never cautious. You fling yourself, all unwary, at the next test, the next confrontation with deadly forces. I cannot be forever looking out for you—and yet I'm terrified to leave you alone. By Thor's mighty hammer, who can say what trouble you'll get into next? I find I don't want to know, don't want to be there when the price of your heedlessness is finally your life."

He fell silent. The room seemed to echo with his words. *Calm,* she reminded herself. *Calm and reason. And honesty.*

"Eric. I'm so sorry I scared you. At this moment I can almost regret that I am who I am, that the time will come when I'll scare you again. But, Eric, what I did today that you hated so much—it worked. And it needed to be done. And I'd do it again, in the same circumstances."

With a low oath, he turned from her. She thought for a minute he would keep going, that he'd grab his boots and his coat and stalk back out the door.

But he didn't. He stopped in midstride—and whirled on her again. "You don't realize, you refuse to understand the magnitude of what lies before us. The danger has only begun. That traitor you forced me to spare today could be the one who kills you in the end."

"Yes," she said softly, "he could."

"Then why in Odin's name didn't you let me cut his throat?"

"Because we didn't *have* to. Because he was already out cold." She ached to touch him. But she wasn't going to make that particular mistake again—not until he *wanted* her touch. She fisted her hands at her sides. "Eric, you just can't do it—can't protect me from every threat. And it's not what I want from you. It's not…what I need. If we're ever going to really be together, you and me, you're going to have to learn to take me as I am.''

He stared at her, his gaze green fire, hotter, somehow, than the red flames in the stove beside her. And then he blinked.

"What?" she demanded. "Say it."

He waved a hand. "It's nothing."

"Don't lie to me, please. Not now. Now I really need you to help me to understand."

He glanced away.

"Look at me. Please..."

He dragged in a breath. "It's only... Someone else said something similar to me recently—that you were not a woman who sought safety, that I would have to learn to accept you as you are."

"Someone else?"

But he only looked at her.

It must have been Valbrand who said it, she thought. The idea pleased her, that while her brother hardly knew her, he understood her so well.

And if Valbrand had been the one, Eric wasn't going to tell her so. She let it go and moved on. "*You've* taken chances—chances that anyone might call insane. Remember, in the camp of the *kvina soldars?* If what you did—walking right into that camp when you knew they might kill you for it—if that wasn't reckless, I don't know what is."

"That risk was well calculated. I knew you were there, knew you would claim me and knew the warrior women to be honorable."

"The risk we took today was calculated, too. And you can't deny that it worked. It gave us information we badly needed. I would do it again in a heartbeat—

and I think you have to get used to the fact that I'm going to keep on doing what I have to do.''

"No," he said, closing the distance between them in two long strides and grabbing her hard by the shoulders.

His fingers dug into her healing wound. She cried out at the sharp stab of pain.

He let go—but only to grab her again, by the arms. The shawl slid to the floor. "I will never get used to it, not if the price could be your life. You almost died today." He spoke low and furiously, his twisted face inches from hers. "That NIB bastard son of a fitz could have killed you." She saw the murder in those burning green eyes.

And the blazing desire.

"Oh, Eric," she whispered. "When will you see? The rules have to be the same for both of us. Or it's no good."

He released her and stepped back. She watched the bright fury drain from his eyes, leaving them suddenly lightless. Dull. "There is no point in this talk. It goes in circles, leading us nowhere. And you leave tomorrow."

"Come with me." The words were out almost before she knew she would say them.

His answer was just what she expected. "It's not possible."

"Why not?"

"You know why not."

She stared at him. It was the closest he'd ever come to admitting that Valbrand lived. "Because of my brother, right? Because he—"

"I cannot speak of it." He put up a hand. "Please. Let it go."

Let it go?

She made a scoffing sound. He should know by now that letting it go was just not her style.

He had to get it through his thick head. Time was running out. They couldn't afford to hang around in the wilds anymore. There were traitors to deal with, a kingdom to save. They needed to go, the three of them, united, to the south. Every day they put off facing their enemies only made their enemies stronger.

It was all there, on the tip of her tongue, what he needed to hear, what she *had* to say.

And then, in a flash of blinding insight, she saw all her righteous arguments for what they really were: cruel taunts, and no more.

Why torment him when she could see the anguish in his now-lightless eyes? Why goad him when at last she understood that she wouldn't be saying anything he didn't already know?

"All right." She spoke softly. "I'll let it go." She crouched to snare the fallen shawl and then stood to her height again, the shawl trailing from her fingers. "I'll just…" She met his eyes again and forgot what she'd been meaning to say.

She was…captured.

By the sight of him, so tall and proud, his ash-brown hair shining in the lamplight, his mouth a bleak line, his jade eyes shadowed and infinitely sad.

She whispered the truth that lay waiting in her heart. "I…oh, God. I will miss you."

A ridiculous flush crept up her cheeks—she could feel it, burning red. Oh, now why had she said that?

Now he would get macho on her again. He'd bark out some surly command: *Then stay* or *Don't go.*

But he only whispered, "As I will miss you."

His stark and gentle words blasted through all her defenses. She heard herself say way too dreamily, "I wish—"

He shook his head before she could get out the rest, the sweetest, most tender of smiles curving the bleak mouth to softness. "Remember, I am but a man. If you tell me your wishes, I will only strive to make them come true."

Astonishing. All their battles, his constant refusal to accept her as she was, and yet at that moment he knew her better than she knew herself. He understood before she did that her wishes and their fulfillment had to be up to her. Well, mostly...

All at once she felt absurdly shy, couldn't even make herself look at him. She stared down at the red knit toes of her socks and didn't know if she dared to raise her eyes again to his. Finally she managed it, though in a shamelessly girly way, glancing up at him from under her lashes. "There is one wish that you could, uh, help me with."

He knew that, too. He understood. She heard it in the quick, indrawn rush of his breath, saw it in the sudden hot light that shone from his eyes. "You're certain?"

She swallowed, nodded. "Even if I can't...be what you want me to be, I've got to have your arms around me. I can't just go away from you tomorrow without..." She let out a small moan. Where were the right words when she really needed them? She dragged the shawl upward, clutched it to her breasts. "Oh, please, Eric. At least for tonight?"

He looked so gorgeously, infinitely regretful. "I am Gullandrian."

No kidding. She gulped. "And that means…?"

"No child of mine will be born a fitz. And I have nothing to protect you from pregnancy. Are you saying that you do?"

Well, as a matter of fact she didn't. She'd come to the Vildelund prepared for action—just not this kind. "Sorry," she muttered, feeling silly and sheepish, "but I don't."

"Then I would want your vow first. Should there be a child from this, you will become my wife."

Her first response was suspicion. Was this a setup? She got pregnant and they got married, as he'd been insisting they were going to do for days now?

No. It didn't add up. If he'd wanted to pull something like that, he would have let nature take its course in Rinda's tent—not to mention in the cave last night, while they waited out the storm. She'd hardly been a shy, blushing flower either time.

Uh-uh. This was no trick. It was only Eric being Eric. Honorable and straightforward…well, at least, about the two of them.

He was offering her the clear chance to back out. If she had any sense at all, she'd take it.

And tomorrow would come and she would go back to the palace. With traitors lurking everywhere, anything could happen. The possibility was achingly real that they would never see each other again—at least, not alive.

Sometimes you just had to go for the old *carpe*

diem—or maybe, in this case, it was the *night* getting seized.

She clutched the shawl all the tighter, a regular Linus response. Next, she'd be sucking her thumb. "Ahem, well. It just occurred to me…" He waited. He wasn't going to help her out at all with this. He was letting it be completely her choice. Big of him. "I mean, well, I guess I have to admit it. Who else would I marry—if I ever do get married—but you?"

He didn't look particularly impressed with her stammered, astonishingly wimpy admission. "No buts," he said. "No ifs. I want your word that, should you become pregnant, you will be my wife."

She had to hand it to him. The guy had no trouble making his position crystal clear.

The least she could do was stand up tall and tell him straight out what she was willing to do. She pulled back her shoulders and dropped her arms to her sides, letting the shawl trail again to the floor. "All right. We're agreed. If I become pregnant, we'll get married."

"You will contact me immediately. We'll be married as soon as I can arrange to come to you."

"Okay. All right. If I get pregnant, we'll get married right away." She still held the shawl by a corner. She let it drop. "So…what do you say?"

He answered without uttering a word, by the simple action of holding out his hand.

Chapter Sixteen

Eric led her to his furs.

They undressed quickly, not quite daring to look at each other, tearing off their clothes and tossing them aside, as if they both feared any hesitation might mean the other would think twice about the wisdom of their actions.

But somehow they made it out of their clothes and, in a scurrying flash of bare flesh and goose bumps, beneath the soft furs.

The bed was narrow, only a smidgen wider than a single. Brit, on the inside, scooted over as close as she could to the rough-hewn wall. She stared at the whirling patterns in the wood and shivered, wondering—though she'd all but begged for this—if it was, after all, a bad idea.

Things weren't really right between them.

And Asta could walk in on them at any time....

Then Eric whispered, so tenderly, "Your sweet body speaks of second thoughts."

She gulped. "Well, yeah." She realized she'd just said that to the wall. She turned her head and there he was—just inches away, smelling of soap and manliness. Looking good enough to eat. She cleared her throat and hated the sound. She'd been doing it so much lately. "Uh, well, we were fighting each other, all day. And we don't know what will happen tomorrow. And now we're here and I..." She didn't know how to finish.

He didn't seem to mind, didn't seem to need her to finish. He canted up on an elbow and gazed down at her, the furs falling away a little. The silver chain slipped to the side, and the medallion dangled along the flexed muscle of his bracing arm, catching somehow a random ray of light and gleaming.

Medwyn had promised the medallion would keep her safe. She sent up a silent prayer that the wise old man had told her the truth when he said that. If the one who wore it was protected, then it would keep Eric safe.

Oh, please, God. Whatever happens, won't you keep this man safe?

Eric touched her forehead—so warm, so right, whenever he touched her—and traced the line of her hair as it fell along her temple and back against the furs. His eyes crinkled at the corners. "Shall I put out the light?"

"No." She forced a smile for him. "It's not the light."

"Then...?"

"Eric...?"

"Yes?"

"Whatever happens..."

He bent close, brushed a kiss at her temple, at the spot where the faintest bruise still remained—where she'd hit her head and been knocked out cold the day her plane went down.

He kissed the tip of her nose, brushed his mouth, too briefly, across her waiting lips.

And she gave him the impossible truth, the one she hadn't known fully until just that moment. "Eric. I love you. I will love you, always. No matter what."

He lifted away—a fraction. And he whispered, "As I love you."

Equal parts joy and sadness swirled through her. She would do what she had to do. But this moment, right now, beneath his furs, naked beside him, their bodies not quite touching, yet still sharing warmth... Her words of love—and his given back to her—no one and nothing could take this away.

He pushed the furs away a fraction. She felt his gaze on her, moving, hungry and tender, along her neck and lower. He bent his head to her left shoulder and pressed a kiss, gentle, lingering, on the white bandage, right over the wound.

With the touch of his lips there, at the warmth of his breath through the white gauze, her sadness vanished.

There was only joy.

She freed her arm from the prison of fur and laid her hand on the warm, hard curve of his shoulder, pulling him closer, moaning a little as his body touched hers, all the way down, in one branding caress.

He had that leather strip tying back his hair. She took it and slipped it off and the silken strands trailed to her shoulder, brushed at her breasts. She let go of the leather strip, had not a care where it fell. He kissed his way along the curve of her collarbone, licked a trail up her throat, over her chin to her waiting mouth.

His tongue dipped in. She drew on it as the medallion pressed itself, warm and heavy, against her upper chest.

He touched her as he kissed her, his hand moving along her eager flesh, leaving waves of longing and delight in its wake. He stroked her arm, learned the shape of each rib, the inward curve of her waist, the swell of her hip...

And lower...

He brushed the side of her thigh.

And then he wrapped his arm around her and rolled until she was on top and he lay beneath her, still kissing her, his lean body a cradle for hers.

She felt him, the hardness of him, pressed at the cove where her thighs joined. It was the most natural thing, to spread her legs and brace her knees to the furs on either side of him.

He groaned into her mouth. And they both went still. She lifted her mouth from his and looked down at him, at his flushed, yearning face, at his eyes, gray-green now as a stormy sea.

She whispered his name. He took her hips and levered her upward, seeking her breast.

He captured it in that tender mouth and drew on the nipple. She felt the wonderful, shimmering shock of connection, as if a thread of sensation pulsed between her breast and her womb. She moaned as his fingers slid over her belly and combed through the curls between her spread thighs.

He found her, long fingers sliding along the wet folds and then entering her. She gasped and then she shuddered. His fingers stroked, so slowly, in and out. The fleshy pad at the base of his palm rubbed knowingly at the center of her pleasure.

She was so wet and so eager. She moaned and moved in a liquid slide against his rubbing hand, at first holding her breast to his mouth and then, unable to go another second without kissing him, bending her legs a little more, taking her breast from him so she could have his mouth pressed to hers.

Another kiss. Endless. Wet. Seeking...

His hand went on stroking, sending waves of pleasure shivering through her.

Until she could bear it no longer.

She reached down and found him and guided him home.

There was a low, guttural moan. His? Hers? Who could tell? The rough, hungry sound echoed in her head. His tongue stroked the wet surfaces beyond her lips.

She lowered herself onto him, inch by slow, delicious inch.

When at last she had him fully, she stilled, her legs folded beneath her, her body holding him, hard and deep. She pushed at his shoulders.

He held her tightly, at first. And then, with clear reluctance, he surrendered. Let her go.

She threw back the sheltering furs and rose above him. He opened his eyes and looked up at her.

"Fearless one," he whispered, the sound ragged and needful and a little bit angry.

She put her fingers against his mouth—to silence him? Maybe.

Or maybe just to feel the hot scrape of his tongue against her fingerpads. She moaned. He sucked her fingers into his mouth, his hips pressing up, as if he couldn't get far enough, deep enough, inside her.

Oh, she could not bear it. She had to move....

She pulled her fingers, dragging, wet, from his mouth, and braced her hands on his shoulders. The medallion had fallen to the side of his neck. It lay, facedown, gleaming, on the furs.

She shut her eyes against it and she began to rock her hips.

They both moaned then. There were hard sighs and soft cries. His strong arms came up and closed around her.

She gave in to him, let him guide her to the side— somehow, he managed it so they remained joined. They faced each other, her outer leg draped over him. He pushed in hard.

She threw back her head and groaned.

He chuckled then—a hot, knowing sound that slid along her nerve endings, striking sparks as it went. She dragged her head back so she could glare at him.

And then she was smiling, too.

And then she *couldn't* smile. She couldn't glare. Her eyes drooped shut and her lips went slack. She could only moan and sigh.

He took her by the nape and pulled her mouth to

his and rolled her the rest of the way until she was under him and he was rocking into her and she didn't care…who was up, who was down.

It was all one, a river of joy and sensation, flowing from him into her and pulsing back again.

She cried out at the finish and he called her name.

There was a silence like snow drifting softly down, a luxurious feeling of floating on air. She was, for that moment, exactly where she wanted to be.

He cradled her close and she snuggled against him.

They were one, as it ought to be.

As it might never be again.

At the hour when the night is darkest, not long before dawn, Asta at last returned to her longhouse. She had her heaviest shawl wrapped tightly around her, yet still she shivered with the cold. Her breath came out as a cloud.

Her steps were heavy with weariness—but her heart was light. A new baby—a girl—was born and cradled in the loving arms of her exhausted mother.

And Brokk—a good boy, that one—had brought the news that Eric and Brit had returned safe and sound.

Asta saw the light gleaming through the narrow slits of the high windows as she trudged up to the door. Were the young people still awake, then? She frowned.

Perhaps having some kind of argument?

They were at odds far too often, in Asta's opinion. Life was so much shorter than the young could ever realize. Young people grabbed every day—and sometimes each other—by the throat.

Of course, it was clear as fresh springwater that Eric

loved Brit and the king's willful daughter loved him back. Still, they had to fight about it, worry their love between them like two greedy dogs with a single bone.

Yes, there were real impediments to their happiness. Brit knew the false story of Valbrand's death for the lie it was. And Eric—like Asta herself—was sworn to vouch for the lie at every turn. It didn't make for trust or easy communication.

That Valbrand. Asta clucked her tongue at the night. Damaged so deeply. And not only his ravaged face. He ought to at least be staying in her longhouse, enjoying the civilized comfort of a sleeping bench and thick furs, eating at her table, where she'd soon put some healthy fat on that too-lean frame.

Instead, almost from the day Eric had brought him to stay in the village five months ago, he'd taken off to live wild, in the woods and in hillside caves, his only constant companion that black horse, Starkavin.

Asta paused at the stoop, reluctant to enter on some moment of discord, straining her ears for the sound of harsh words.

She heard only silence within.

With a small sigh of relief she pushed open the door to the warmth of the fire and the light of the lamp, which waited on the table, burning low.

And what was that? A lump of wool on the floor...

She recognized her old gray shawl. But where were the young people?

Ah.

With great care, so as not to disturb them, Asta shut the door. Her weariness had vanished, her body was no longer cold. Wearing a look much too soft and full of dreams for a woman who'd raised her sons and set her husband's funeral boat afire, she started back up the street.

There was always a sleeping bench for her at Sif's. Or at Sigrid's, for that matter....

Chapter Seventeen

Brit woke to daylight. She turned her head to see Eric, already up and dressed, spooning bowls of steaming oatmeal from a cast-iron pot.

He glanced her way and smiled. All of last night was there, in that smile. In those deep, knowing eyes.

God, she hoped she wasn't blushing. Her cheeks felt way too warm. She sat, raking her hair back from her forehead and pulling the furs with her to cover her bare breasts—which was kind of silly, if she thought about it. It wasn't as if he hadn't already gotten an up-close-and-personal look at them.

At all of her, for that matter.

"Come," he said. "Eat."

"Ahem." Oh, great. Throat clearing again. She had to stop doing that. "Where's Asta?"

"At Sif's." How did he know that? Did it matter?

Probably not. He set the pot on the stove and went to the counter by the deep, old-fashioned sink.

As soon as his back was turned, she leaned over and snatched up her long johns from where she'd dropped them the night before. Under cover of the furs, she wiggled into them.

When Eric turned around again, she was perched on the edge of the bench, pulling on her socks.

"Gotta make a quick trip outside."

He nodded, poured himself a cup of tea and sat down to eat. Brit slid on the clogs Asta had loaned her, grabbed the gray shawl from the peg where somebody had hung it and went out into the brisk, bright morning.

She was back in no time. She went to her own sleeping bench and got a bra from the pack beneath it. Turning to the wall, she pulled her arms out of her shirt and put the thing on. She added her jeans and sweater over the long johns and then ran a brush through her hair.

Well, hey, wow. Ready to face the day.

More or less.

She washed her hands and joined Eric at the table. They ate. They cleared off and washed their bowls and cups and spoons. She was setting the second bowl in its place on the shelf when he touched her—a breath of a touch, the back of his finger to the side of her throat and gone.

"At night, a temptress. In the morning, a little anxious—and trying to pretend that she's not."

She felt a smile quiver across her mouth. "Oh, Eric..." She set the towel on the counter and turned to him.

He gathered her into his arms.

It felt really good to be there. She nuzzled his warm neck and breathed in the scent of his skin and tucked her head against his strong shoulder. "What are we going to do about us?"

He held her away a little so he could look down at her. "Do you really want me to answer?" She didn't, and they both knew it. He took her hand and pressed it to his chest. She could feel the round shape of the medallion beneath his heavy wool shirt. He gave her his answer, whether she wanted it or not. It was only one word. "Stay."

The crazy, insane truth was, she wanted to do exactly that. She could admit that now, for all the good it did. But...

"You can't," he said, finishing a sentence only begun in her mind. "You have set yourself a task and you will see it through, no matter how bitter the end."

She looked deep into his eyes. "And you should be with me. You know that you should..." He started to speak. She put her fingers to his lips. "Never mind. Believe it or not, I kind of understand. My brother needs you near him. And you won't desert him."

He caught her hand again and kissed the pads of her fingers, one by one. "I never said that."

"It's all right. I forgive you."

He was frowning—but playfully. "Did I ask for your forgiveness?"

"It doesn't matter. You have it, anyway." She pulled her hand free of his gently. "I hope it keeps you warm at night when I'm not here."

He smiled at the taunt. "Your mouth is forever uttering barbed words. I like it better when you use it for kissing." He tipped his head down.

She tipped hers up.

And there. Her mouth was doing what he liked—kissing him. Actually, she liked it, too.

A lot.

With a long sigh, she slid her arms up his broad chest and wrapped them around his neck so she could stroke his nape and toy with the idea of pulling the leather cord from his silky hair.

She never got a chance to decide if she would do it. He lifted his head too soon. "I've contacted your father with our plans."

She pushed at his chest and his arms dropped away. "You contacted him by shortwave?"

"Yes."

"I am a little curious about this shortwave setup I've never seen that you're always sending my father messages on."

"Gunnolf has a work shed behind his and Sif's longhouse. We have it rigged with a generator. The radio is there. I suppose you'd like to see it?"

"Not really. I just wondered where it was." She stepped back. "And what, exactly, are these plans of ours?"

"We'll leave as soon as you're ready, you and I, on horseback. We'll go through the Black Mountains, by way of the Helmouth Pass."

The Helmouth Pass. Such a charming name.

She knew where the pass was. At least, she'd seen it on the map. It twisted through the mountains, beginning about twenty miles south and slightly east of the village.

Eric went on, "The mountains are still passable. The snows have yet to close them off. We'll stay about midway through the pass, high in the mountains, in a traveler's hut I know of, for tonight. By tomorrow, at late morning, we'll be on the other side. Your father is sending Hauk Wyborn to meet you and accompany you the rest of the way to Isenhalla."

"I gotta ask, whatever happened to the option of a nice, efficient helicopter? Seems like a helicopter could easily land in one of the pastures out back—and I could just climb on and be at the palace in no time."

He looked very serious. "You'd prefer that, then?"

"I'm just saying, it seems a lot simpler."

"Good enough." Did he sound…too casual? "Would you care to come with me while I send a second message?"

She studied his face. Yeah. Way too guileless. "What's going on?"

"I thought you would perhaps want to take your horse with you. But if you prefer the helicopter, I promise you that Svald will be well cared for here."

Her horse. Right. "Eric, is there some valid reason you can't tell me what you're up to here?"

Now he was the one studying her. And frowning. Finally he admitted, "I suppose not…beyond the usual unswerving desire to protect you—thoroughly misguided, at least in this case. My apologies." He was so handsome when contrite. "We very well could get through the mountains without incident. Still, you should understand the danger."

"The bears and the mountain cats, right? And let's not forget all the fine young renegades and—I think

I've got it. The biggest threat of all. That would be the bad guys with the guns who call themselves NIB.''

He shrugged. ''And there you have it.''

''Traveling overland, we get to be bait.''

He nodded. ''So you see? Here I am, suggesting that you put your life in danger. After this you must never again accuse me of trying to keep you safe.'' He spoke teasingly. He was making a truly valiant effort to keep things light.

But she saw in his eyes what he didn't say. Should they meet up with Jorund's men, there was a very good chance she'd never again be accusing him of anything.

It's hard to do much accusing when you're dead.

Chapter Eighteen

Asta and her family—Sif and Gunnolf, and Sigrid and her husband Brokk the elder, and all the little Borghilds—came out to say goodbye. There were hugs all around.

Little Mist instructed, "Bwit. You come back soon."

"I will," she promised, feeling only the slightest twinge of guilt that it was a promise she had no idea if she'd be able to keep. She looked up from the child into Asta's worried eyes.

"I don't like this," the old woman said. "The pass through the mountains is dangerous. And why must you leave us so soon?" Brit had no answer for her. She held out her arms. With a grunt of disapproval, Asta allowed a second goodbye hug.

"Thank you," Brit whispered against the old woman's thick white hair. "For everything..."

"Humph," said Asta. When Brit let her go, she fumbled in the pocket of her skirt and came out with a kerchief. "Oh, now—" she dabbed her eyes and blew her nose "—you keep safe. You hear me?"

"Absolutely, Asta. I will."

She caught Eric's reproachful look as she mounted her horse. Well, and what was she supposed to say? He swung up into the saddle as Asta chided him, "Take care. Keep well...."

They started off along the dirt lane in the opposite direction from the way they'd gone two days before. Brit turned to glance back more than once. Each time she looked, the Borghilds remained in the middle of the dirt street, waving goodbye. Gunnolf had lifted Mist to his shoulder, and the child's small frame rose above the rest. She had her plump arm held up, her tiny hand swaying back and forth.

Too soon they reached the trees. The Mystic settlement—and the small knot of well-wishers—was lost to view.

They reached the next village to the south two hours later. It looked much like Asta's village: a single dirt street lined with matching rows of longhouses, pastures and barns and livestock pens spreading out behind the houses to the edge of the trees.

Brit remembered what Asta had told her that first time she woke from her fever—that her guide's body had been sent to his family in a village to the south. "Is this the village where Rutland Gottshield's family lives?"

Eric gave her a bleak look. "We haven't time to linger here."

"Only for a moment. I'd just like the chance to pay my respects."

"Be quick."

He led her to the second house on the left side of the street. A woman, her long red hair streaked with gray, came out to meet them. Brit introduced herself and explained that she'd only come to offer condolences, that they couldn't stay, had no time even to come inside. The woman, Rutland's widow, who said her name was Trine, saluted, fist to chest, in the Gullandrian way and spoke of how honored she was that Her Highness had stopped. Trine said the king had seen to her well-being and the future of the four sons—working in the pastures now, and out hunting—who had lost their father. She murmured shyly that she would forever mourn her husband, but knew great pride that he had died bravely in the service of his king.

In her mind's eye, Brit saw Rutland's pale face and shaking hands when they had boarded the Skyhawk. "Yes," she told the widow. "Your husband died a hero's death." Her next words came to her, stolen from the stories she'd heard at her mother's knee. "May he feast and fight forever in Odin's great hall."

The widow stood in the street, waving, when they rode away. Brit glanced back once and thought of the Borghilds, waving, as they'd left Asta's village. She had a strange, sinking feeling. As if she and the man beside her rode toward something huge and horrible, as if they were leaving all kindness and goodwill behind.

The way was much easier than the trip into Drakveden Fjord—at least at first. The hills sloped gently, with small valleys between. The road, well traveled, lay before them wide enough to ride abreast.

No bands of renegades attacked them. Mountain cats and bears kept to the shelter of the trees off the trail. If traitors lurked nearby, it must have been only to watch and wait for some later opportunity.

They stopped briefly for a quick meal of jerky and trail mix at noon. About an hour later they reached the base of the jutting, jagged mountains crested at the highest points with white, and began climbing. Soon the trail narrowed. The steep black cliffs soared up and up on either side, the sky a slice of blue between them. Eric took the lead.

They rode mostly in shadow. The sunlight couldn't reach them between the high rock walls. The wind kicked up, whistling down on them. And clouds began to gather.

So inconvenient. Brit could almost start to feel that Mother Nature didn't like her much. Every time she had someplace important to go lately, the weather had to up the stakes. She pulled her beanie down more securely over her ears and hunched into her jacket— which, as usual, she didn't dare zip up all the way as she'd have poor access to her weapon.

Most of the time they were traveling south, protected somewhat by the rock walls around them. But when the trail jogged north, they headed into the wind. The cliff faces on either side made a tunnel through which the icy air rushed at them hard and fast as a runaway train. Brit's lips went numb, and her chin ached with cold. She worried that her eyeballs would freeze in their sockets. She marveled at her own idiocy; she could have brought a damn ski mask, for goodness' sake.

And then—but of course—the snow started to fall, stinging flakes that beat against her cheeks and gathered on her eyebrows. She got the hood free of her collar and pulled it up, tightening the strings and tying them beneath her chin with gloved hands that felt like slabs of ice. It didn't help a whole heck of a lot. But it did keep the snow from slipping in around her neck.

The snow came down thicker—well, maybe *down* wasn't the word for it; it swirled around them on the angry wind. Brit gave up on the weapon-ready angle and zipped her coat to the neck. Her fingers were so cold and stiff she doubted she could deal with her gun right then, anyway.

They went on forever, into the cold, blustery white, sometimes moving down into a steep canyon or a rocky gorge, but mostly, it seemed to Brit, moving ever upward toward the stormy sky and the high cliffs that rose tauntingly above them.

Okay, all right. She wasn't as tough as she liked to think she was. She'd have ordered Eric to stop a hundred times by then, if there'd only been anywhere *to* stop. But the snow was piling up on the trail and there was zero shelter that she could see. If they stopped, they'd probably end up freezing to death.

They went on.

For hours. Sometimes the snow abated and there was only the freezing wind. But it always started up again.

The snow was blowing at her again, thick and white and blinding, when she pulled back her sleeve and checked her watch. Nearly seven. It must be getting dark. But who could tell? The clouds above were so thick and black, the cliff walls so steep around them, it had seemed like the middle of the night since about three in the afternoon.

And then, out of the stinging white and the howling wind—shelter. Around a sharp turn, in a little cove of flat land to the side of the snow-white trail, an old wood shack materialized, silvered with weathering, out of the storm.

Brit had never in her life been so thrilled to see four walls and a roof. And was it possible? Could that be a stone chimney she saw on top of that beautiful roof? A chimney would mean a fireplace, and a fireplace just might mean...

Oh, be still, my beating heart.

Eric led her around to the most protected side, facing the cliff. A crude porchlike structure consisting of a roof and side walls, about ten feet deep and covering the entire cliff-facing wall, led into yet deeper shadow.

They slid from their horses to the snow-covered ground and went beneath the shelter of the roof.

Eric handed her his reins. "Watch the horses. I'll only be long enough to get the fire started."

The fire...

Then that *had* been a chimney. And if there was going to be a fire, she would literally melt with gratitude. He opened the door on the wall of the shack, stepped in and shut the door.

The horses snorted and shook their snow-thick manes. More good news: the snow slid right off and left them hardly wet at all. Less work for her and Eric. Oh, yay, hooray! Plus, it wasn't nearly as bad standing here as out there in the storm. Pretty darn cold, yes.

But bearable. The horses would be fine out here. And there were railings suitable for hitching to either side of the door.

And speaking of the door—it wasn't set in the frame all that straight. Golden light glowed around the edges of it. Oh, yes, yes, yes!

The door opened. Eric stood there, holding a lighted kerosene lamp. Behind him, on the side wall, the fire in the fireplace was already crackling away.

They unsaddled the horses, brushed them down quickly and fed them the oats Eric had brought outside. Then they lugged their gear inside, where the cheery fire was blazing, and Brit dared to hope she might actually get warm again sometime very soon.

The one-room shack had two doors: one led to the shelter where they'd left the horses. The other, on the wall opposite, faced the trail—two doors, no windows. Like the cave the other night, the shack had been stocked with the bare necessities. The furniture wasn't much: a small table and a couple of roughly made ladder-back chairs.

Eric took one of the chairs and braced it under the knob of the door that faced the trail. "It won't stop anyone," he said, "but it will give us a little warning." The door they'd come in through opened out. Bracing a chair against it would accomplish nothing. Eric must have caught the direction of her gaze. "It's doubtful they'll use that door, anyway, too much chance they'd spook the horses and give us warning."

"If things get crazy, they'll probably be coming at us from both sides."

He didn't argue. "We'll put the table against that one, then."

He put out the lamp and set it in the corner with the blankets and the bucket, the can of lamp oil and the bag of feed. They positioned the table, legs out into the room, against the lean-to door. It wasn't big enough to reach the top of the door frame—but, hey, they had to make do with what was available. Once the table was in place, they spread their bedrolls before the fire. They sat, backs against their saddles, to eat their dried meat and oatcakes.

"Shh," Eric said a while later. "Listen."

Had he heard boots in the snow? Brit felt a shiver, like ice water trickling down her spine. She whispered, "I don't hear anything."

He saw her wide eyes and smiled. "Easy. I only meant the wind has died. The storm is passing. We'll have a clear day tomorrow, I'd lay odds on it, and no more than six inches of snow on the ground. It should be passable."

She let herself slump against her saddle. "And not a peep from Jorund and crew."

"The night is young."

She stared into the dancing flames of the fire. "I suppose, if they're out there, the smoke from our chimney will lead them right to us."

He gave her a wry look. "That *is* the idea...."

"So we...keep our weapons close and our eyes open?"

"Well said." He had his rifle beside him. "They'll fall on us—or they won't. We'll live. Or we'll die."

A licking warmth tingled through her—and not from the fire. At last he was accepting her as an equal, someone he trusted to be ready, willing and able to fight at his side. She could almost get starry-eyed.

"Be ready," he said softly.

She sent him her best come-and-get-me smile. "I will."

He reached across the distance between them, wrapped his warm hand around the back of her neck and pulled her toward him. Their lips met in a hard, hungry kiss. He whispered against her mouth, "I would like nothing better than to drive you wild with pleasure tonight—and increase the odds you might be forced by your own vow to marry me."

"Hmm. We're back to the breeding issue again, are we?"

He let out a long, aggressively rueful sigh. "But, alas, one should never get undressed when under the threat of being set upon by traitors."

"Oh, I don't know. It sounds kind of…exciting."

"Too exciting. And distracting. Plus, it's discouraging to be attacked while naked."

"Happened to you before, has it?"

He chuckled. "Not recently, no."

"I have to admit I'd rather die with my boots on."

"Then keep them on. And get back into your jacket."

"I suppose next you'll say I have to keep my shoulder rig on, too."

He nodded. "You want to be ready to defend yourself—and ready to run, too. And that means you'll need—"

"Outerwear. All of it."

"That's right."

Another thought occurred to her—a not-very-pleasant one: *the Freyasdahl signs.*

Ho-boy, now there was an issue she really should have considered last night.

The Freyasdahl signs had been named by her father, when her mother, who had been a Freyasdahl, experienced them, though the signs came down through the women in her family...

Which got way confusing and wasn't the point. The point was, when a woman in her family got pregnant, she also got the signs within twenty-four hours. First, she threw up, and then she fainted and then a bright red rash would appear across her chest. Brit had been there when it happened to her oldest sister, Liv.

But really, the chance that might be happening to her in the next few hours had to be minimal, didn't it?

Yeah, right. Ask Liv about that. She'd gotten pregnant after one wild night with Finn Danelaw....

Eric was watching her. He read her too well. He knew something was wrong.

Why, oh, why hadn't she thought of this last night?

Well, hey, last night she hadn't realized that tonight she'd be holed up in the Helmouth Pass waiting for a gang of traitors to bust in the door.

She didn't want to tell him. It was one more thing to worry about, and there were far too many of those already.

But if the signs did put in an appearance, they could be grossly inconvenient. He needed to know there was a remote possibility that she'd be throwing up and fainting in the middle of the part where they were fighting for their lives.

"Ahem," she said.

He regarded her for a moment. "I fear that doesn't sound encouraging."

"Well, it's like this..." She told him, in as few words as possible. When she was done, she added sheepishly, "I just...thought of it and realized you should know."

He took her hand and kissed the knuckles. He did have the softest lips in the world. "Put it from your mind."

Hah. "Sure."

"It's only one dire possibility among so many."

He had it right there. "Eric?"

"Yes, my only love?"

"How many would you guess there are going to be?"

"It depends on how good they think they are. There could be only one or two—trained and experienced assassins—to slip in on us and cut our throats. Or perhaps the six, from the crash site..."

"And what about my *friend*, Agent Sorenson?"

"Ah yes, possibly Agent Sorenson as well. They'll have horses, perhaps leave one to tend them. And they could leave another one or two outside, to stand guard."

"So what you're really saying is, you haven't a clue how many there'll be."

"Yes. That's what I'm really saying."

"Are we crazy to be doing this?"

"Oh, yes. Beyond the darkest shadow of a doubt."

At a little after midnight Eric told her to try to get a little sleep.

Great idea. Get some sleep. Be fresh when the assassins arrive. "What about you?"

"Later. I'll wake you and you can have your turn on guard."

"Goody."

"Sleep."

"I can't bear not to ask…we do have backup, don't we?"

He answered with a wide smile. "We do."

"I guess I don't get to ask who?"

He only looked at her and softly repeated, "Sleep."

To be a good sport about it, she settled against her saddle and shut her eyes.

Unbelievable. She must have actually dropped off.

Because the next thing she knew, Eric's hand was on her shoulder. "They come…"

There was a clattering noise—the chair at the door.

Brit sat bolt upright, going for the SIG.

Eric had already turned and shouldered his rifle. His first shot exploded, deafening in the small space, as the chair gave way and the door flew inward.

A man, his features covered by a ski mask, fell half into the room. Another came after him. Eric fired and he fell back, out of sight, into the darkness beyond the doorway.

There was silence—one awful, endless second of it.

And then a voice from the back door said, "Drop your weapons or die."

Chapter Nineteen

There were two men at the back door, one with a rifle and one with a combat pistol. They'd used the confusion of the frontal attack to open the door and get themselves in place. The table, smaller than it should have been and still right where she and Eric had put it, covered them both to chest height. Like the others—the man who lay, too still, in the doorway and the one who had fallen back—they wore ski masks over their faces.

"Set your weapons on the floor. Do it now."

Eric sent her a glance, an almost-imperceptible nod. Together they crouched and set their guns down.

"Now stand up. Hands high."

They obeyed. Brit's heart pounded as if it had plans to escape from her chest. She hadn't gotten off a single shot. And why the hell hadn't she had sense enough to cover the other door? Things had happened too damn fast. Next time—if there was one—she'd know better.

And hey, wow. At least she wasn't throwing up and fainting. She did kind of have that whoopsy feeling in her stomach. But the Freyasdahl signs had nothing to do with it.

That was pure terror talking.

It was her first gun battle. Her performance? Far from impressive. But at least she and Eric were still breathing—for the moment, anyway. She glanced at the fallen man in the front doorway and knew a twinge of regret—mostly that she couldn't help being glad he was probably dead.

"Safe to enter, sir," said the man with the rifle trained on them. About then the man in the front doorway pushed himself up, groaning. Not dead, after all, though he didn't look too healthy. His face had a bluish cast and things looked real bad at about belt level. Gut shot. She'd seen a lot of action movies. Gut shot was not a fun way to go.

He fell backward, groaning, into the night behind him.

Another man—about five-seven and powerfully built—appeared from the darkness and came through the wide-open front door. He stood opposite Eric and aimed his pistol right at him. Yet another, taller and leaner, followed after him, crossing behind him to take a position opposite Brit. Both, like the two in the back doorway, were armed.

Four men, in combat boots and camo, ski masks covering each face. Four guns, all trained on Brit and

Eric. Brit's pulse showed no signs of slowing down soon.

The short, beefy one—whom Brit had already recognized by his height and build and the confident way he carried himself—reached up and yanked off his mask to reveal his shaved head.

A bullet of a man, she'd thought the first time she saw him. Compact and deadly—but with such a winning smile. Weeks ago, which seemed like centuries now, she'd sat across from him at Loki's Laughter, the homey neighborhood pub near the Bureau offices that the agents liked to frequent. With a tall glass of sweet Gullandrian ale on the scarred oak table in front of her, she'd told him her theories about what might have happened to her brother, tickled pink with herself to have been so clever as to cultivate a connection with him.

"Hello, Jorund."

Special Agent Sorenson grinned, showing straight white teeth and a lot of friendly laugh lines. "Your Highness. So good to see you again—though I'm certain you're *not* pleased to see me. But then, it's your own fault. You should have killed Hans here when you had the chance." The man beside him took his left hand from his rifle just long enough to drag off his mask and let it drop to the floor. Good old Hans Borger.

Hans wasn't smiling. He had her in his sights again, just waiting for the order to blow her head off—the order that, she had a sinking feeling, would be coming very soon.

Jorund had more to say. "Fortunately for me, Princess, you are too softhearted. You let Hans live. And, once he was through babbling nonsense about a legend come to life, he remembered that you had seen him that first day you visited my office and thus would be…oh, how to put it? 'On to me,' now. And with you 'on to me,' well, I knew that it wouldn't be long before the king's soldiers came knocking at my door. I found it expedient to come looking for you before you had a chance to speak with your father.'' Jorund indulged in a little cheerful chuckling. He appeared to be having a very good time. 'A legend come alive?' He must mean the Dark Raider. Valbrand must have paid Hans a visit after she and Eric left him yesterday.

Jorund turned his ice-blue eyes to Eric and clucked his tongue. ''Radio messages…so easy to intercept.'' He gestured at the two still-masked agents waiting at the back door. ''We'll take over here. Stand guard.'' They lowered their weapons, backed into the shadows and were gone.

Brit really hoped that the backup Eric had mentioned would be showing up shortly. In the meantime, well, nothing ventured… ''Who do you work for, Jorund?''

Jorund found her so amusing. He chuckled some more. ''Questions, questions. Your Highness has always asked far too many questions. And what good will the answers do you now—on the night of your death?''

''Hey, you know, just wondering.…''

Jorund tipped his head to the side, considering. ''Well, and then again, why not? A tidbit or two— before Hans dispatches both you and Prince Greyfell. This is really too, too good. To be rid of you both in one night. Together, you know, you represent a very large threat to the plans of certain important people. Should you be allowed to live and perhaps to marry, and thus unite your two houses…'' He shook his head. ''Disaster. Prince Greyfell, here, would in that case most assuredly be named our next king.''

Brit shrugged. She was proud of that shrug. It was cool and offhand and spoke nothing of the way her stomach twisted and her pulse raced. All she had to do was *not* look at Eric, not let herself even think that in a few minutes he could be dead. If she didn't look at Eric, she could do this. ''But then again, if we're dead, we can't get married.''

Jorund indulged in another jovial chortle. ''Your Highness, you astound me with the brilliance and clarity of your powers of deduction. You've cut right to the heart of the matter.''

''These important people you just spoke of—they want the throne?''

Jorund was clucking his tongue again. ''Well, now, *someone* has to claim the throne when the next king-making occurs. Sadly, both Thorson princes are dead. After tonight, there'll be no Greyfell to step forward. *Someone* must take over. And the kingmaking could come at any time—some would say, sooner than you'd think….''

Brit used her brilliant powers of deduction. ''You're planning to assassinate my father.''

''Not to worry. That won't happen for a while yet. He'll have time to suffer and mourn some more first— over another child gone forever. How very, very sad.''

''Valbrand? You're responsible for that, too?''

Jorund heaved a big, fake sigh. ''So unfortunate. Lost at sea. Just as you and Prince Greyfell here will be lost, vanished forever in the Helmouth Pass.'' He gestured at Hans, who had his rifle pointed at Brit's heart. "Ready?''

"Yes, sir.'' Hans spoke flatly, still sighting, finger ready on the trigger. This close, Brit was going to have a very big hole in her chest. The irony was perfect. It was just as Eric had predicted.

She'd spared the agent's life—so he could be the one to kill her.

"And now, Princess, I'm afraid it's time to bid you fare—''

Something thudded against the north wall of the shack. Both Jorund and Hans glanced back toward the sound.

It was all the opening they needed. Eric dived for Jorund. Brit went for Hans.

Weapons fired and shots went wild—ricocheting off the stone fireplace. Brit managed to knock the rifle out of Hans's grip as it fired. He let it go—and dealt with her.

It was a fight she knew she couldn't win. Sure, she'd had a few self-defense lessons. But Hans was bigger and stronger and combat trained. Hand-to-hand, he would take her. She tried to kick him where it mattered, but he was ready. He jerked his hips away and then threw a leg over her, trapping her beneath him. In a split second he was looming above her. His fist connected—hard—with her jaw.

Spots spun and danced before her eyes. He hit her again. Her head bounced against the floor.

She saw double—Hans shifting and fading in and out of himself, two right fists coming at her at once. She knew she was done for.

And then a sound like the world coming apart—a shot.

Hans had a red hole in the center of his face. Blood was spraying everywhere. He collapsed on top of her, his ruined face smacking the floor above her bad shoulder a few inches from her head, sending more blood spattering. Dazed, bloodied, her suddenly limp would-be murderer pinning her to the floor, she saw Eric standing a few feet away, her own trusty SIG in his hand.

She blinked, because everything still kept going double, and behind Eric...

Valbrand—minus the Dark Raider's mask, his poor face as she remembered it, a horror on one side—in the doorway. Valbrand had a gun, too. He had Jorund in a neck lock, the gun pointed at his head. Valbrand was backing out, dragging Jorund with him.

"Brit." Eric filled the world as he crouched beside her. He pushed the limp man off her. She looked up into his face, her head spinning, her heart aching—but aching in a *good* way, really. Because he was alive and she was alive, at least so far. Because she'd just seen her brother, alive, too, and not hiding behind a mask.

She blinked as she heard a sudden soft roar. She lifted her head, blinked again.

What was this?

The fire had...escaped. It was a bright ribbon, eating up the floor, sizzling out from the fireplace.

How could that be?

"Come. Now." Eric held out his hand. She put hers in it. He pulled her up.

She swayed on her feet. The room went round and round and the flames...

They were licking at the old, dry boards of the floor, creeping ever closer. Smoke curled up, billowing. She coughed as Eric wrapped a strong arm around her and half dragged her to the open door.

They stumbled over the sill. She fell—but he caught her and dragged her up again, up and away from the flames, out to the snow-thick trail.

At last. Safe. She sucked in a great breath of the cold, fresh night air. Eric's strong arm was tight around her, holding her up. She clung to him, so tight. They watched the shack burn.

Her dizziness slowly faded. She looked at Eric. His eyes blazed, reflecting the flames. "The fire...how?"

"The lamp oil. I kicked it over when I grappled with Sorenson. The lid must have come off."

"Hans..."

He gave her a dark scowl. "Dead. You saw his face. His blood is all over you. Don't you dare ask me to go in there and pull his body out."

"I'm not. I promise." She huddled against his warmth and shook her head, trying to clear it, to understand it all. Then she turned enough to gape at the empty doorway beyond which the bright flames danced. "The two men you shot...when they first burst through the door?"

A voice from behind her said. "Wounded but alive. One might even survive. The other, shot in the belly, most likely not."

Eric released her. She swayed a moment, then steadied. She turned, slowly, her heart kicking hard against

her ribs, knowing that voice though she'd heard it only
once, when she was so ill. "Valbrand."

Her brother nodded.

With a glad cry she took one step and then another.
At the last minute, her brother held out his arms.

Chapter Twenty

As the shack burned, the flames licking high toward the last of the night, Valbrand led them around to the back, near the face of the cliff, where Gunnolf and Brokk the elder and two other strong men from Asta's village were waiting with the horses. At their feet a row of traitors, Jorund among them, lay bound in the snow.

"It is important work we've done tonight," Gunnolf announced with pride. Svald, as if in thorough agreement, tossed her braided mane and let out a joyful whinny.

Brit turned to the brother she'd found at last. "And now what?"

He smiled. It was a hideous smile—and the second most beautiful she'd ever seen. "We go, with the daylight, all of us together, to the south. There are traitors to bring to justice. And our country to save."

It was exactly what she'd hoped, schemed—and nearly died—to hear. For tonight there was only one more thing that needed settling.

She turned to the man at her other side. "I wonder, could we have a moment...just the two of us, alone?"

Brit and Eric left the others and went back, hand in hand, around the front of the blazing shack.

They stopped, of one accord, at the place they'd stood before, on the trail, opposite the glowing rectangle of the open front door. They watched the consuming flames, the sparks shooting high into the darkness, bright spots drifting down, winking out into ash.

Eric wrapped an arm around her and pulled her close to his side. "The night seems black as ink now." He breathed the words against her blood-matted hair. "Yet dawn will be on us in the wink of Odin's good eye."

Keeping tight in the circle of his strong arm, she turned until she was facing him, sliding her arms around his waist to link at the small of his back. With a long sigh, she leaned fully against him—the best place in the whole world to be—her head on his shoulder, her heart so close to his.

She breathed in the scent of him: smoke and sweat, the blood of their vanquished enemy. "Oh, Eric. All I wanted was to find my brother. And I did—and so much more...."

He caught her chin, tipped it up. She winced—her jaw was way tender, from Hans's deadly attentions. "You've blood in your brows, on your cheeks, in your lashes. And you'll be black-and-blue from ear to ear.

And yet, as always, you are so very beautiful.'' Behind her, the fire roared. The flames danced in his eyes.

"My dad will freak when he sees me."

"The blood will wash off. And the bruises will heal."

"They'd better. I want to be lookin' good when I hand you my wedding sword."

His brows drew together—though he was smiling. "Could this mean…?"

"Oh, yes. It most definitely could."

"And since you have neither been sick, nor fainted—"

"Well, I came pretty close to both, when I was sure we were done for—and then when Hans started punching me. But that was stark terror and a couple of mean right hooks."

"So. You don't carry my child."

"Not if I'm like the rest of the women in my family—and anyway, it doesn't matter. I don't want to marry you because I'm pregnant. I don't want to marry you because it's supposed to be fated. Or because it could strike a telling blow against the enemies we haven't even routed out yet. Oh, no. I want to marry you because—'' She sighed, swallowed. Now, where had the words gone?

He waited, knowing she would find them.

And she did. "Because I love you. Because you're the guy I've been waiting for when I didn't even know that I *was* waiting."

"As I have waited, only for you."

He bent his head. She lifted hers. The kiss was long and so very sweet. It pushed back the night and warmed the snowy mountaintops.

When they moved apart, it was only so he could take the medallion from around his neck and settle it over her head.

"Forever," he said.

"And always," she whispered.

He smoothed the silver chain, pressed the medallion in the place it was meant to be, near her heart. Then he took her hand again and twined his fingers with hers.

They turned to the fire as the shack gave way, collapsing inward with a heated rush. Sparks shot skyward, a million tiny points of hot light that, winking, fell. Hungry red flames licked higher, a moment of false triumph—then faded downward to the rubble with a sound like a surrendering sigh.

And in the east, the sliver of paleness along the rim of the mountains signaled the coming day.

* * * * *

And what of Valbrand? Does his return to the kingdom mean he will receive the crown? Don't miss THE MAN BEHIND THE MASK, coming from Silhouette Books in May 2004 to a bookstore near you.

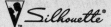

SPECIAL EDITION™

Secret Sisters...

Separated at birth—in mortal danger.
Three sisters find each other and
the men they were destined to love.

International bestselling author

Annette Broadrick

brings you three heartrending stories
of discovery and love.

MAN IN THE MIST

(Silhouette Special Edition #1576)
On sale November 2003

TOO TOUGH TO TAME

(Silhouette Special Edition #1581)
On sale December 2003

MacGOWAN MEETS HIS MATCH

(Silhouette Special Edition #1586)
On sale January 2004

Available at your favorite retail outlet.

Visit Silhouette at www.eHarlequin.com   SSESS

Your opinion is important to us! Please take a few moments to share your thoughts with us about your experiences with Harlequin and Silhouette books. Your comments will be very useful in ensuring that we deliver books you love to read.
Please take a few minutes to complete the questionnaire, then send it to us at the address below.

Send your completed questionnaires to:
Harlequin/Silhouette Reader Survey, P.O. Box 9046, Buffalo, NY 14269-9046

1. As you may know, there are many different lines under the Harlequin and Silhouette brands. Each of the lines is listed below. Please check the box that most represents your reading habit for each line.

Line	Currently read this line	Do not read this line	Not sure if I read this line
Harlequin American Romance	❏	❏	❏
Harlequin Duets	❏	❏	❏
Harlequin Romance	❏	❏	❏
Harlequin Historicals	❏	❏	❏
Harlequin Superromance	❏	❏	❏
Harlequin Intrigue	❏	❏	❏
Harlequin Presents	❏	❏	❏
Harlequin Temptation	❏	❏	❏
Harlequin Blaze	❏	❏	❏
Silhouette Special Edition	❏	❏	❏
Silhouette Romance	❏	❏	❏
Silhouette Intimate Moments	❏	❏	❏
Silhouette Desire	❏	❏	❏

2. Which of the following best describes why you bought *this book?* One answer only, please.

the picture on the cover	❏	the title	❏
the author	❏	the line is one I read often	❏
part of a miniseries	❏	saw an ad in another book	❏
saw an ad in a magazine/newsletter	❏	a friend told me about it	❏
I borrowed/was given this book	❏	other: _____	❏

3. Where did you buy *this book?* One answer only, please.

at Barnes & Noble	❏	at a grocery store	❏
at Waldenbooks	❏	at a drugstore	❏
at Borders	❏	on eHarlequin.com Web site	❏
at another bookstore	❏	from another Web site	❏
at Wal-Mart	❏	Harlequin/Silhouette Reader	❏
at Target	❏	Service/through the mail	
at Kmart	❏	used books from anywhere	❏
at another department store or mass merchandiser	❏	I borrowed/was given this book	❏

4. On average, how many Harlequin and Silhouette books do you buy at one time?

I buy _____ books at one time	❏
I rarely buy a book	❏

MRQ403SSE-1A

5. How many times per month do you shop for any *Harlequin and/or Silhouette* books?
One answer only, please.

1 or more times a week ☐	a few times per year ☐
1 to 3 times per month ☐	less often than once a year ☐
1 to 2 times every 3 months ☐	never ☐

6. When you think of your ideal heroine, which *one* statement describes her the best?
One answer only, please.

She's a woman who is strong-willed ☐	She's a desirable woman ☐
She's a woman who is needed by others ☐	She's a powerful woman ☐
She's a woman who is taken care of ☐	She's a passionate woman ☐
She's an adventurous woman ☐	She's a sensitive woman ☐

7. The following statements describe types or genres of books that you may be interested in reading. Pick *up to 2 types* of books that you are most interested in.

I like to read about truly romantic relationships	☐
I like to read stories that are sexy romances	☐
I like to read romantic comedies	☐
I like to read a romantic mystery/suspense	☐
I like to read about romantic adventures	☐
I like to read romance stories that involve family	☐
I like to read about a romance in times or places that I have never seen	☐
Other: _____	☐

The following questions help us to group your answers with those readers who are similar to you. Your answers will remain confidential.

8. Please record your year of birth below.
19 _____

9. What is your marital status?

single ☐   married ☐   common-law ☐   widowed ☐
divorced/separated ☐

10. Do you have children 18 years of age or younger currently living at home?
yes ☐   no ☐

11. Which of the following best describes your employment status?
employed full-time or part-time ☐   homemaker ☐   student ☐
retired ☐   unemployed ☐

12. Do you have access to the Internet from either home or work?
yes ☐   no ☐

13. Have you ever visited eHarlequin.com?
yes ☐   no ☐

14. What state do you live in?
_____

15. Are you a member of Harlequin/Silhouette Reader Service?
yes ☐   Account # _____   no ☐

eHARLEQUIN.com

For **FREE online reading,** visit
www.eHarlequin.com now and enjoy:

Online Reads
Read **Daily** and **Weekly** chapters from
our Internet-exclusive stories by your
favorite authors.

Red-Hot Reads
Turn up the heat with one of our more
sensual online stories!

Interactive Novels
Cast your vote to help decide how these
stories unfold...then stay tuned!

Quick Reads
For shorter romantic reads, try our
collection of Poems, Toasts, & More!

Online Read Library
Miss one of our online reads?
Come here to catch up!

Reading Groups
Discuss, share and rave with other
community members!

For great reading online,
visit www.eHarlequin.com today!

INTONL

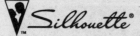

COMING NEXT MONTH

SSECNM1003